THE BRICK MAN 5

Lock Down Publications and Ca$h
Presents

THE BRICK MAN 5

A Novel by *King Rio*

The Brick Man 5

Lock Down Publications
P.O. Box 944
Stockbridge, Ga 30281
www.lockdownpublications.com

Lock Down Publications
Like our page on Facebook: Lock Down Publications @
www.facebook.com/lockdownpublications.ldp
Book interior design by: **Shawn Walker**

Stay Connected with Us!

Text **LOCKDOWN** to 22828 to stay up-to-date with new releases, sneak peaks, contests and more…

Thank you!

Submission Guideline.

Submit the first three chapters of your completed manuscript to ldpsubmissions@gmail.com, subject line: Your book's title. The manuscript must be in a .doc file and sent as an attachment. Document should be in Times New Roman, double spaced and in size 12 font. Also, provide your synopsis and full contact information. If sending multiple submissions, they must each be in a separate email.

Have a story but no way to send it electronically? You can still submit to LDP/Ca$h Presents. Send in the first three chapters, written or typed, of your completed manuscript to:

LDP: Submissions Dept
P.O. Box 944
Stockbridge, Ga 30281

DO NOT send original manuscript. Must be a duplicate.

Provide your synopsis and a cover letter containing your full contact information.

Thanks for considering LDP and Ca$h Presents.

Dedications

This book is dedicated to the everlasting memory of Terrineka Jones, who was instrumental in the creation of several characters from the *Mobbed Up* and *The Brick Man* series. Cancer may have taken you from our eyes, but you'll forever be in our hearts.

And also to "Bean", the 11-year-old literary prodigy whose school writing project absolutely blew me away. As I told that strong Black mother of yours, you are beyond exceptional. I hope you continue writing stories, so that one day the world can see just how brilliant that mind of yours truly is.

Acknowledgements

I have to give a huge shout out to Ca$h and the entire LDP roster of urban fiction authors. Ca$h, thanks for everything, big dog. We've only just begun.

To my family in Chicago, I love y'all with every drop of blood in my heart. Y'all know this street shit will be in me till judgement, but I got a good heart, and I miss you all too much to describe in words. I'll be back home very soon. Until then, keep me in your hearts and prayers.

To the bros on lock, stay focused. Keep learning. Get to that bag if you can, but no matter, what be sure to feed your mind with as many books as possible, whether they be fictional or educational. Each one teach one, you know. Shout out to my bro Lil B for suggesting the subtitle for this book. Shout out to Demetrius "Young Meach" Burks, and definitely to Stephen Hannah, who paid for my TV when I got to the SHU free of charge even though he knew I had it to buy my own. To all my 22-12 bros, Mighty on that! (Inside talk.)

Contact me on Facebook at: Author Rio

Instagram: @authorrio5

Email: authorrio@gmail.com

King Rio

Chapter 1

It was December twenty-eighth.

Sincere Jerrell Owens and his lovely wife, Tamera, were sitting in Rell's pearl white Mercedes, which Tamera had just parked across the street from St. Sabina Church on the south side of Chicago.

"This is a terrible idea," Tamera said, slowly and haltingly. "If Mila walks out of there and sees us, she'll know something's up. And besides, what are you gonna do when somebody gets in that truck? You can't just start shooting. There will be dozens of eyewitnesses. We'll both end up in jail."

Rell considered it, then nodded. "Yeah. You're right. I just wanna know who owns the truck and see where they live. We'll follow it from here."

"To the burial? You want me to join a funeral procession? Did you even *try* to think this through?"

Why the hell didn't I think this through? Rell asked himself sternly, and replied in the same mental breath: *Because I didn't know for sure if the truck would be here. Not for sure, anyway.*

Jamal Cushenberry's funeral service was underway inside the church. He was a sixteen-year-old who'd been murdered on the west side six days ago over death threats he'd made against Rell's younger brother, Jahlil, who was now in Northwestern Memorial Hospital, recovering from five bullet wounds he'd suffered in a shooting two days after Jamal's murder.

The man who'd shot Jah had arrived to and departed from the shooting scene in the black Dodge Ram pickup that was now parked at the curb in front of the church. It was obviously the same pickup. If the Indiana plates didn't give it away, the bullet holes along the driver's side of the pickup did. There were a few of them in the fender, several more in the driver's door, and seven or eight in the side of the truck bed.

The funeral service had begun at 10:00 a.m., approximately an hour and ten minutes ago, and Rell knew that it was almost over.

Tamera had called the church and learned that there was another funeral scheduled to begin at noon.

"We should've come in a different car," Rell said, realizing he'd rushed into this situation without much planning. He looked down at the Tec-9 submachine gun on his lap, studying the ventilation holes in the barrel. "I wasn't thinking at all, was I?" He chuckled once.

"I don't think you were," Tamera said.

"I just want the nigga who shot my li'l brother."

"That's understandable. But you have to be smart about it. I love you with everything in me, but I refuse to spend the rest of my life in somebody's jail because my husband was too angry to think things through. You might as well put that gun away. I'm not about to let you shoot up a funeral procession, and I'm not about to drive in one, either."

"So I'm supposed to let this nigga get away?"

"Right now, yes." Tamera turned to look at Rell, her jaw working ceaselessly as she chewed a stick of minty chewing gum. She had on a white Moncler sweater, designer jeans, and the shoulder-length blond hairstyle that all of her friends were wearing, and she looked even more beautiful than she had on their wedding day: dark-skinned, curvy, and impossibly sexy.

Rell didn't look bad himself. He was a good-looking young black man in a black hoodie and sweats. He was remarkably handsome - all the girls said so - but he wasn't what you might consider a pretty-boy. He was more rugged than anything, a walnut-hued realtor who was normally laid-back and attentive. For the majority of his youth he'd been a wild young gangbanger, but a stint in prison had calmed him down. Since tying the knot with Tamera, he'd been focused on building his real estate empire, using drug money to renovate his homes, and then renting them out. But he'd put all his business on the back-burner when Jahlil was gunned down. Now all he could think of was revenge, and obviously he wasn't thinking clearly.

He lifted his eyes from the gun and settled them on the Dodge Ram. It was parked about ten feet behind a gleaming black Cadillac hearse. There was a large photo of Jamal Cushenberry on the inside of the hearse's back window. Several grief-stricken family members were standing at the bottom of the long, red-carpeted concrete stairs, smoking cigarettes, impervious to the biting cold.

"Hand me your phone,'" Tamera said suddenly.

"For what?"

"Just give it to me." She unwrapped another stick of Doublemint chewing gum and folded it into her mouth, then dug in her pink Chanel bag and pulled out a roll of scotch tape.

Reluctantly, he handed over his iPhone. The thirst for revenge was beginning to nibble at his nerves. He lit a Newport and drew deep, relishing the way the smoke slid into his pipes, as everyone headed back inside to say their final good-byes.

Tamera pushed open her door and took off across the street before Rell could even register what had happened. She left the driver's side door hanging open. Rell concealed the Tec in his sweats and stared after her, wondering what the hell she was doing. She was right up on the black Dodge Ram, beside the rear driver's side wheel. She squatted down on her haunches and reached under the truck.

Rell gaped at her, momentarily incapable of thought. He swept his eyes up and down the street, doing a quick attendance check — so quick it was almost unconscious. There were a few characters farther south: an elderly white man with fine white hair and red blotches on his cheeks; a young black woman with thick glasses, a narrow face, and long straight black hair.

He caught movement in the corner of his eye, and before he could swing his eyes back to the front of St. Sabina, a newcomer had turned the corner of the building and begun mounting the church steps.

It was James Cushenberry, Jamal's older brother. He had his head lowered against the cold, hands buried in the pockets of a long black trench coat. Tamera came trotting back to the car just as James was entering the church.

She got behind the wheel, snatched her door shut, and let out a huge sigh. Rell looked at her with wide eyes. He had lowered his window an inch or so to let out the smoke; a snowflake slipped in through the narrow opening and fell on the back of his hand, and another fell on the clean white paper of his half-smoked cigarette.

"Where in the fuck is my phone?" Rell asked.

Tamera shifted into drive and pulled away from the curb. "It's taped to the underside of the truck. We'll use the GPS tracker to follow it after the burial. It'll lead us right to whoever shot your brother," she said. "Let's just hope my gum and a few strips of tape are enough to hold the phone in place."

Rell smiled. "My better half," he said gratefully. In his current state of mind, he knew that he would not have been able to come up with a plan of any sort, most assuredly not one as simple and effective as the one Tamera had just set in motion.

Had it been left up to Rell, he would have just waited for the pickup's driver to come out of the church, walked up on the guy, and shot him dead. Now the man who'd shot Rell's brother would live a little longer. Lucky him.

Chapter 2

Bubbles opened the door, and Juice was very taken with what he saw. Before him was just about the most perfectly turned-out woman he had ever seen. She was dressed in her standard uniform of Chanel dress, Ferragamo shoes, plain gold jewelry, and a gold Rolex wristwatch and bracelet. Her hair was done in a neat blond bob, and not a strand was out of place.

"Juice got the juice," Lakita "Bubbles" Thomas said, offering him a cheek to peck. She turned and led him into the living room, a vision of soft colors and good pictures.

Following in her footsteps brought the sweet scent of her fragrance to the nostrils of Lee "Juice" Wilkins. His eyes lingered on her gently swaying hips as she walked in front of him, then moved up to her smooth caramel shoulders before plunging back down to the thick round swells of her ass.

"Love that perfume," Juice said, knowing he was saying the right thing.

"Thank you, kind sir," Bubbles said.

"Love you even more."

"For that, you get a real kiss," she said. Bubbles took his face in her hands and planted upon his lips a soft kiss, with only a hint of tongue. Her carefully applied lipstick remained unsmeared. "And now for a drink," she said, and headed for the mini bar, her tall heels clicking and clacking across the hardwood floor as she went.

"No ice, please."

"Jack Daniels? Remy Martin? Hennessy?"

"Henny gang in this thang."

"I should have known," she said. "Brown is all you drink."

"That Henny is my medicine."

"I'm just glad you're not popping pills and drinking Lean," she said, deftly pouring two drinks at a wedding table across the room. "You look good in that suit, by the way. Never thought I'd see you in one of those."

"I wear suits only when I'm in the presence of strippers named Bubbles," he said, and chuckled as he lifted his drink.

"To strippers," Bubbles said, raising her glass.

"I'll drink to that."

They did.

Bubbles took his hand and led him to the sofa. "I hope you're not about to tell me there's been another shooting," she said.

"Not yet."

"Good; I'm in no mood for bad news." She studied his black suit and gold tie. "What kind of suit is that?"

"Canali. I actually wore it for a meeting I just had with my lawyer and this real estate agent a few blocks down from here. I got the house for the twins. They can move right in whenever Dawn gets back from Jamaica."

"You plan on selling the building on Drake?"

"Nope. Renting it out once I get the front door replaced," Juice said. He sat back and sipped his cognac. "Your guy is flooding me with new clientele. Guys from all over have been blowing up that phone he gave me. I just got rid of a hundred bricks to some young nigga in St. Louis. Last night, the same amount went to some cat from Cleveland. About an hour before that, a nigga named Spradley sent two chicks in from Indianapolis, and that was *another* hundred bricks gone. I sold twenty of 'em to Grindo on Christmas, twenty-five of 'em to Bowlegs, and Reese bought *another* hundred. I knew he wasn't lying when he said he would send some clientele my way, but it'd be a lie to say I expected the money to come this fast."

There was a gleaming oval coffee table of burled walnut in front of them. Bubbles picked up her iPhone from it and thumbed her way to the calculator. Behind her cool expression was a layer of excitement not even her makeup could conceal.

"How much are you charging for each kilo?" Bubbles asked.

"Taxing everybody twenty-two bands a brick this go around."

"And how many have you sold so far?"

"Four hundred and…fifty-five. Yeah. Four hundred and fifty-five of 'em, because Luke just bought ten."

Bubbles calculated. Her jaw dropped, and she gasped. The excitement burst through the cool, and she turned to Juice. "Are you kidding me?" she said, her tone pitched a few notches above normal. "That's over ten million dollars, Juice!"

"I know how much it is."

"You can pay Blake off right now and sell all the rest for profit."

"I *could*. Not going to, though."

"Aren't you glad you listened to me and left that gang life alone? Now look at you. You're on top. You just made over ten million dollars in less than a week's time and you hardly had to lift a finger. None of this would have been possible without me. Don't ever forget that."

"Do you have to take credit for everything?" Juice asked, taking another stinging swallow of Hennessy.

"No, not everything."

"Where's your evil little demon?"

She laughed. "My daughter is not evil. My sister took her to see a movie. *Fences*. That new movie with Denzel in it. I heard it's a good film."

"We'll go and see it tomorrow."

"So why'd you tell me to be dressed and ready to go out?"

"Because we're going out." Juice leaned forward and set his glass down on a rubber coaster. "It's a double date. That's all I'll say."

"Nah-uh. I don't do surprises. Tell me who we're having dinner with, or you can just go by yourself."

"You don't wanna do that."

"Why not?" Bubbles squinted at him over the rim of her glass, a sexy squint she tended to put on at least ten or twelve times daily. "What are you up to? Who are the other two people? Is it Kev and Tar? Reese and Shawnna? Rell and Tamera?"

"Speaking of Rell and Tamera," Juice said, grinning, "Rell was supposed to grab ten bricks off me — I told him, Jah, and Wayno they could get 'em for fifteen racks a piece — but he's so focused on finding the man who shot Jah that he ain't even thought about coming to shop with me. He called me from Tamera's phone a few minutes ago saying he had found the black pickup truck."

"The one from when Jah got shot up?"

Juice nodded. "It was parked outside the church at Jamal's funeral. He had Tamera tape his iPhone to the damn truck. Can you believe that? They're using GPS to follow it now."

"Why won't he just pay one of the Vice Lords to do that?" Bubbles asked, looking and sounding worried. She dialed Tamera's number without waiting for an answer from Juice, and seconds later, she was on the line with Tamera.

Juice sat back, but found he couldn't relax - at least not completely. Part of it was because his home in the North Lawndale neighborhood on Chicago's West side had been the scene of not one, but two shootings — one on Christmas Eve morning, the other on Christmas Day — at a time when his gang was already under heavy surveillance from the Chicago Police Department. Part of it was because his daughter Shawnna had been the target of the second shooting, and the fact that one of the gunmen had gotten away was a little unnerving. And part of it was because he had been fronted a thousand kilograms of cocaine two days before Christmas, and he was more paranoid than ever. Chicago was ending the year 2016 with almost eight hundred murders, more homicides than Los Angeles and New York combined, and the soaring body count was garnering national attention. In Juice's opinion (and probably everyone else's), Chicago was the absolute worst city for a drug kingpin to reside.

One wrong move and I'll be living next to Larry Hoover.

An unpleasant thought, but one that was hard to dispute. He had crossed a line last week when he had made a deal with the wealthiest gangster rapper in all of hip hop. He supposed he had known at least that much, but it wasn't until today that he had realized how final that line was, how small was the chance of his ever being able to cross back to the other side of it again. To the *safe* side.

No, he couldn't relax. At least not yet.

Bubbles ended the call, put her phone back on the table, and turned to Juice with wide eyes. "They're really doing it," she said, her voice pitched to the heights of disbelief. "Tamera is literally on I-94, chasing down a phone signal like some kind of FBI agent."

16

"You thought I was lying?"

"I'm not sure what I thought. I'm just hoping they don't get themselves into something they can't get out of. Those two are so perfect together, you know? They should've just paid somebody to do that."

"Rell took it personal when Jah got shot," Juice reasoned.

"All the good couples are going through hell this month. First Shawnna found out her man got her best friend pregnant. Tirzah found out about Jah and Mila. Blake left Alexus for the picture she took with T-Walk. And now the nicest married couple we know is on the hunt for some old man in a black pickup truck. What the hell is going on?"

"Kilograms and heartbreaks, baby," Juice said, lifting his glass. "That's what's going on."

King Rio

Chapter 3

Tamia Thomas was twenty-one years old, and she usually went after young black men her age. In fact, she had not had sex with anyone under the age of eighteen since her high school years.

But today was different.

The man she'd been sexing for the past few weeks – a tall, dark, and handsome high-ranking Vice Lord named Wayno – had been stolen away from her by Dawn Wilkins, the daughter of the man who was currently dating her big cousin Bubbles. Now Dawn and Wayno were together in Jamaica, having the time of their fucking lives in a Ritz-Carlton hotel suite, and Dawn was using social media to rub it in Tamia's face. Dawn was continuously uploading photos and videos of her and Wayno's great Jamaican adventure to Snapchat, Instagram, and Facebook. It was enough to make Tamia grit her teeth every time she thought about it.

Which was why Tamia had just parked her brand-new Chevy Equinox in the alley behind Dawn's ex-boyfriend's house on St. Louis Avenue. His name was Cage, and when Tamia had messaged him on Facebook asking if she could come over and chill, the seventeen-year-old had immediately agreed.

Tamia was a small woman, just 4'11" tall, with a cute pie-shaped face and a big round butt. She had made a stop at the liquor store and bought a bottle of Patron and an orange juice. She hopped down from the driver's seat wearing a pair of tight faded jeans and a Georgetown University T-shirt, beneath which she was clearly braless. Cage came down from the back porch and grabbed her bag of drinks and her purse while she put on her blue leather Cubs jacket.

"This truck yours?" Cage asked. He was dark-skinned and about five inches taller than Tamia. His cuspid teeth were chipped in a way that made the empty space look like someone had forced a miniature pyramid between them. He licked his dry lips and shouldered her driver door shut. His hair was cut low and seemed to have not been brushed or greased in days or weeks.

What the hell did Dawn see in this ugly-ass nigga? Tamia thought, eyeing the ragged holes in the left shoulder of his plain red hoodie.

"Yeah, it's mine," she said, shadowing him to the back porch. "I just got it this morning. It's spanking new. Twenty-seventeen." *Unlike your aging hoodie. Twenty-fourteen.*

"You hit me up at the right time," Cage said. "My mama just went to work about twenty minutes ago, and she took my son to his mama when she left. I got the crib all to myself."

"Lucky us," she said with a cheerful grin. It was a grin that a man could fall in love with, if he wasn't careful. "Are you even old enough to drink? I brought a whole bottle of tequila. Don't tell me I gotta drink it by myself."

"I'm grown as hell," Cage said, and grinned back at her. "My room's in the basement. We can chill down there. I got a pool table. Only one stick, though."

They hurried up the steps to the porch of the small frame house and slipped inside. Tamia caught just a whiff of Pine-Sol in the air. Then she turned back to Cage, caught him staring at her ass, and smiled.

"It's all real, nigga," she said

Cage looked at her appraisingly. "I already know." He paused, then added, "You're thick like your cousin Bubbles."

"Runs in the family."

"I'll tear your li'l thick ass up."

"Oh? Is that so?"

Cage flashed his chipped teeth as he kicked the door shut. "When I moved out of my bedroom and into the basement, the basement turned into the Red Room," he said. "Come on, let's go down."

The kitchen and the hallway beyond it were dark. The light – along with a murmur of trap music – was filtering up the steep staircase to their left.

They descended with Cage in the lead – the staircase was too narrow for them to walk abreast – and passed through an open doorway into a well-lit, low-ceilinged basement room that probably ran

20

the length of the rickety old frame house above. There was a large bed in the back, a pool table with balls scattered all across it in the middle of the floor; a red-carpeted section to the far right where five folding chairs were set up, and a huge TV with an Xbox One connected to it hung on the whitewashed brick wall before them. Around the chairs were ashtrays and Xbox controllers. Tamia was amused to see a framed picture on the left-hand wall, with a sign reading THE RED ROOM: ENTER AT YOUR OWN RISK! Beneath it.

"Well, I've entered," Tamia said, her smiling face aglow with the threat of a laugh. She had gotten her hair dyed blond and shaped into a long bob, because Bubbles had a short blond bob and she looked up to Bubbles.

Cage chuckled once. He retrieved a sleeve of red plastic cups from atop a black mini fridge that stood next to the bed, then they sat down in folding chairs. He filled two cups with tequila and juice while Tamia fired up a blunt she'd rolled earlier. A Young Jeezy music video was playing on the TV. Tamia watched it as she inhaled with obvious relish.

"I see you done came up," Cage said, and sipped his drink. "Hair done, nails done, new truck. You still working at that restaurant?"

"Nope. I quit." She streamed smoke out of her nostrils. "I started dancing at Redbone's two days ago. This'll be my third night. I've already made over two grand working there, and I made about the same amount for some runs Juice had me make."

"What kind of runs?"

"I can't tell you that. You wouldn't want me telling your business, would you?"

"I'm only asking 'cause I need a job. I ain't been able to make no money since my uncle got caught up in that raid on Spaulding earlier this month. He was supposed to be putting me on once he got back right, but somebody killed him last week. I can't get no more bread from my OG 'cause she's paying for most of his funeral. My baby mama was helping me a little, but now she's fucking with some new nigga. I'll work for Juice if that's what it takes to put some money in my pocket."

"Why don't you go up there to McDonald's and put in an application? I heard they're hiring."

Cage shook his head. "I don't have a diploma, I don't have a GED. They ain't gon' hire me," he said, taking the blunt.

"Okay." Tamia didn't know what to say to that.

Cage chuckled, shrugged, and looked defiant, all in the same instant. "Shit, I'll get it one way or another. I used to stick niggas up when I first moved over here with my old girl. I kept money back then. That's the only reason Dawn started fucking with me in the first place. She knew I kept a knot in my pocket. Now I'm all fucked up again. But that won't last long. Mark my words. I'll be back on my feet soon. The important thing, the only thing I have to get straight and keep straight, is that I got a three-year-old son that I *have* to take care of. I gotta keep him with school clothes, toys, food, medicine…" He paused, thought it over, and shook his head. Now he looked and sounded like a man holding a conversation with himself, trying yet again to answer some question which has held him sleepless over too many nights. He raised the blunt to his chapped lips and drew deeply, allowing Tamia to note that the knuckles were gray with ash.

"Fuck Dawn. You don't need a gold-digging bitch like her anyway. If she won't stick around when you're dead broke, then you don't need that bitch. You need a rider, the kinda bitch that'll put you on your feet when you don't have the means to do it yourself. A boss bitch. Dawn and Shawnna might have their own hair salon and all that, but money ain't everything. If you ain't loyal, you ain't shit."

"You're right about that."

A pause ensued. Young Jeezy gave way to Solange Knowles. Outside, the wind whistled against the high cellar basement window, but down where Tamia and Cage were, it made only a strange muffled humming that was not quite a vibration.

"To be honest," Tamia said, continuing her rant against the Wilkins twins, "Dawn's a gold-digger just like Shawnna. I mean, look at who Shawnna got pregnant by. She's pregnant by the richest young nigga in the city. Bankroll Reese actually *owns* Redbone's."

"And The Visionary Lounge."

"Exactly. Ex-fucking-zactly. But guess what? Joke's on her, because that nigga got Myesha pregnant too. Both of their dumb asses are four months pregnant. And Dawn's trying to get on the money train now. She's in Jamaica with Wayno, and everybody knows Wayno is getting big money working for Juice. Before him she was fucking Luke, the music producer who manages Grindo. He produced 'Thumb Through It', that song Grindo made with Durk and Herbo."

"That's dumb," Cage said, and offered her a hard, humorless grin. "Why would Dawn fuck with a nigga who works for her pops when she can just go to her pops for money?"

"Because she wants a cut from both ends. Because she's money-hungry just like her pregnant-ass sister," Tamia said, leaning forward with her eyebrows raised. "Don't act like you're surprised, Cage. Please don't act like you're shocked by the shit. You know damned well that she would still be all on your dick if you still had that car on rims. When Juice was in jail and she was broke, she went everywhere you went. Now tell me I'm lying."

Cage's mouth shifted into a smile. His eyes shone with a look of total fascination – a look similar to the look at pot-bellied trucker named Daniel had worn when Tamia gave him a lap dance at the strip club last night. There was a twitch in the crotch of Cage's sweatpants. Tamia spied the jump in her periphery as she was lifting her cup. The sweat pants were of a darker shade of red than the hoodie, and newer.

"Last I heard," Cage said, passing her the blunt, "you and Wayno was messin' around. All this shit you're talking about Dawn wouldn't happen to have anything to do with her and Wayno being together, would it? Because that's the vibe I'm getting."

"No, it doesn't."

"Sure sounds like it."

"Well," Tamia said, and snatched the blunt from between his pinched thumb and forefinger, "you need to clean out your ears."

"I just got out the shower before you got here."

"That explains a whole lot," she muttered under her breath.

"What's that supposed to mean?"

"That you're supposed to put on lotion…and hair grease…and a little Chapstick wouldn't hurt."

Cage threw back his head and laughed. Then he got up, shaking his head, and crossed the room to the cluttered dresser that stood against the back well on the far side of his bed. "I didn't have time to get all the way together before you showed up. That's my bad."

"For a minute there I thought I was looking at Tyrone Biggums, that crackhead from the *Dave Chappelle Show*."

"You got me fucked up."

"Thought you might've had skin cancer," Tamia said, flashing her dangerously seductive grin as she slipped out of her jacket and slung it over the seat of a vacant folding chair. "You scared me."

She refilled her cup, watching him take off his hoodie and undershirt. Holding the half-smoked blunt and her cup in one hand and her smartphone in the other, she got up and headed toward him. Her eyes fluctuated from the glass screen of her phone as she thumbed her way to Snapchat, to Cage's reflection in the dresser mirror as she observed him rubbing the lotion on his arms and chest. Her inner whore wondered if his *dick* was ashy.

She stood next to him, leaned toward him. Her breasts pressed against his elbow as she kissed his smooth, ash-less shoulder, which was moist and soft now. On the outside, at least. Underneath the skin, there was hard muscle. He didn't have a six-pack, but he wasn't exactly out of shape, either. He greased and brushed his hair and all of a sudden he was…well, he was…fuckable. That was the word. Fuckable.

Tamia put her smartphone in her back left-hand pocket and then leaned her hip against the dresser. Cage took the blunt and puffed, then picked up his cup and drank, studying himself in the mirror.

"Was the job you did for Juice a lot of work?" Cage asked. "You can at least tell me that much."

"Why are you so interested in knowing my business?"

"Because I'm broke, and two bands would change my life right now."

Tamia hesitated. The liquor was working in her bloodstream. It felt like her brain was in a blender. Her nipples were stiff. She could feel the juices flowing in her heated nether region. "I, uhh…I rented a U-Haul truck and delivered some boxes to some people, a few different people."

"That's it?" He looked at her, brows raised.

"That's it."

"He paid you two thousand dollars to deliver some boxes?"

"Yep. That's all I did. I picked up the boxes from an apartment in K-Town the first two times, then dropped them off at different places. Just regular cardboard boxes."

"You don't know what was in 'em?"

"No. I didn't ask. I just made the pick-ups and deliveries, got my money, and went on about my day. I'm not into questioning the people who pay me. That's not a smart thing to do." Her eyes were cast down at the front of his sweatpants, which was poking out so far she could actually see into them through the opening at the front of his waistline.

Tamia set her cup down on the dresser and snatched his sweatpants and boxer briefs down to his knees – she couldn't help herself. His dick sprang free. It was about seven or eight inches long and insanely thick, curved slightly to the right. She curled her fingers around it and looked up at him. One of his dark hands moved under her T-shirt and up to her breasts. Left and right it traveled, as if uncertain which breast it wanted to settle on.

"You gon' eat my pussy first?" Tamia asked.

"Hell no," Cage said – and was that petulance in his voice? She thought it was. This was a Cage she had never even suspected. "I know how you get down, Tamia. You fuck niggas like niggas fuck bitches."

"That's so sexist."

"No, it's not."

"So it's cool for you to fuck fifty bitches, but I'm trifling if I fuck twenty niggas? That's messed up. Bitches get horny too. And besides Wayno, I ain't fucked another man in almost two months."

"That's not a long time."

Tamia sucked her teeth, grinned, shrugged, and then pushed Cage's shoulder with the heel of her hand. "Sit down, I won't bite."

Cage didn't look so sure of that. Nevertheless, he sat down on the side of his poorly-made bed, caressing her cheek as she spit on his fat erection — as it turned out, his dick actually *was* ashy — and began stroking it in her hands. She squatted down between his open legs; legs that looked like they'd been rolled in powdered sugar, and jerked his dick.

"I like to swallow," Tamia said, looking up at him, "so don't try to skeet on my face or on my ass. Make sure it's in my mouth when you bust every time. Can you do that?"

"What kind of question is that? Hell yeah I can do that."

"I'm just letting you know so we don't have any misunderstandings. I paid two hundred dollars for these eyelashes and four hundred for this hair, and I'll be damned if I let some nut mess it all up." She reached back for the bottle of lotion, squeezed a dollop of it onto the palm of her hand, and rubbed his legs until they were no longer powdered.

"How can you be so sexy," Cage said, "have the biggest booty in the world, and yet at the same time be the biggest *freak* in the world? How does that work? Because I don't understand it."

"Women like sex just as much as men do," Tamia said, lotioning his balls now. "Men are considered cool when they act on it, you know, when they fuck a bitch they're *really* the man. Women are supposed to be classy about the shit. We're supposed to be in relationships all the damn time, cooking and cleaning for a nigga who's out there fucking every hoe under the sun. But I'm not that bitch. I do it like you niggas do it. If I feel like sucking and fucking, then that's exactly what the fuck I'm going to do, and I ain't ashamed to say it. Right now I'm tipsy off that Patron and I feel like fucking and sucking on you. Is that a problem?"

"Definitely not." He leaned back on his elbows, smiling.

"Okay then."

There was nothing more to say.

Tamia cupped his heavy scrotum in one hand and held his dick in the other as she took the head into her mouth and slowly began to suck it in and out, twirling her tongue around it, already antici-pating the salty drink she would take from it in the end. The only thing she enjoyed more than getting her pussy eaten was the taste of cum shooting onto her tongue when she was sucking a fat black dick. Cage was bald between the legs, which meant his girlfriend or whoever he was having sexual relations with these days probably enjoyed sucking dick just as much as Tamia did.

Just thinking about Cage's cum was enough to bring Tamia close to an orgasm. She had once read that the taste of a man's se-men varied depending on his diet, that if he ate a lot of fruit and drank a lot of water and didn't smoke cigarettes, his cum would taste really good. But none of that mattered to Tamia. She loved to swallow cum, no matter how fresh or bitter it tasted. The only thing she hated was sucking a dick until her jaws ached and only getting a few drops of cum for her efforts. She liked it as thick as Elmer's glue. The more the better. And if she could suck out one or two more cum loads in the same session, she would do just that. About a week ago, she had gotten so turned on when Wayno came in her mouth that she'd actually had an orgasm as she was swallowing it all down.

Her oral sex skills were the talk of North Lawndale for a reason. She knew how to twist and turn a dick in her hands while at the same time sucking it tightly in her mouth. She knew how to prolong a man's climax and also how to expedite it. She could deep-throat like a sword swallower, even when the dick was gushing out semen. She didn't do it that way often, though. She preferred having just the head in her mouth when the cum came out, so that she could get the full taste of the semen and swish it around in her mouth before letting it drop down into her tummy.

Cage lasted only eight or nine minutes. Then a long, halting grunt crawled out of his throat, and he clamped a hand onto the side of her head. With his thumb pressed just below her left eye, his fore-finger pressed halfway into her ear, and his last three fingers on the side of her neck, he exhaled sharply through his nose and injected her mouth with a tangy dose of semen.

She gulped and smiled.

Chapter 4

It was a wet, dreary afternoon and the Benz's radio clock had just made half past two. Rell sat in the passenger's seat, his eyes darting restlessly about, cataloguing everything, although there was precious little to see on Interstate-94 today.

"I wonder why it stopped there on Franklin Street for so long," Tamera said in a low, inquisitive tone.

The beacon on Tamera's iPhone told them that Rell's phone was in Michigan City, which was about a fifty minute drive from Chicago. Rell's phone was in Michigan City, Indiana, which was about a fifty minute drive from Chicago. Rell's phone had lingered on Franklin Street in Michigan City for over thirty minutes before continuing on to Southgate Apartments, where, according to the tracking beacon on Tamera's phone, it still remained.

"Probably was a stop at the gas station," Rell said. He had Tamera's phone and was looking at the place where the beacon had lingered on Google Earth. There was a Marathon gas station there, a Moose Lodge — whatever the hell that was — a preschool, and, one block over, a train track, a pottery shop, a bar on the corner, and several other shops.

Tamera shook her head, "We should be at the hospital with Jah," she said drably. "Not out here in Michigan City, Indiana."

"Tirzah's at the hospital with Jah," Rell said.

"We should be there with them."

"No, we should be right where we're at now, looking for the person who put him in that hospital. If you don't wanna stay here, you can go home and I'll just find this nigga myself."

"You know that's not even an option."

"Then leave it alone and drive," Rell said snappishly.

"Watch your tone, Rell. I understand you're upset, but I'm not about to let you take your frustration out on me." She glanced over at him, a suggestive smirk playing around the corner of her mouth. "Not unless you *really* take it out on me. That's about the only way I'll put up with that kind of talk."

Rell opened his mouth to speak, only to discover he was too angry to say anything. The image which kept returning to his mind was that of his younger brother lying in a blood puddle on the sidewalk with holes in his jacket. Then there was the image of the shooter in the black Dodge Ram, a dark-hued man with close-set eyes and thickly braided cornrows that were almost completely gray with age.

It was a face Rell would not forget.

Rell pulled a cigarette out of his pack of Newports and lit up without doing Tamera the courtesy of lowering his window a crack. He'd only fallen off the wagon four days ago, and already the inside of his year-old Mercedes had the sallow, yellowish odor of tobacco smoke. The nicotine soothed his troubled mind immediately, so much so that he actually chuckled at himself.

"So," he said thoughtfully, puffing his cigarette, "is that what you want me to do? You think getting out my frustration that way is the answer?" His eyes gleamed skeptically through a rising ghost of gray smoke.

"I believe," Tamera said quietly, "that it is."

"We'll test out the theory as soon as we get back home to Chicago," Rell remarked, and he handed over her phone before returning to his ceaseless catalogue of the highway through which they passed. "We should be back by six or seven at the latest."

They were on an off-ramp that curved up and around to an overpass which led directly into Michigan City. The Mercedes rode so smoothly that it seemed to float up the ramp. Rell finally cracked his window. Chilly air swept into the car, knocking a roll of ash from his cigarette.

"When Jah gets out of the hospital and heals up a little," Tamera said, glancing at Rell again, "she's filing for divorce. She told me earlier, said she's tired of the cheating. I can't say that I blame her. If you cheated on me, I'd be out the door so fast you wouldn't know what happened."

"I wouldn't give you the satisfaction," Rell said, smiling.

"Can you believe that T.I. and Tiny are getting divorced? I meant to tell you that too. Saw it on The Shade Room this morning."

"What the hell is up with you and The Shade Room? Is it like TMZ for black people or something?

"Yeah, pretty much. Actually, it's better than TMZ. It's more personal, in my opinion. Even the celebrities are on there. You can see them commenting under the photos all the time. Oh, and something else I saw on there today – Bulletface and Alexus aren't living together anymore. I guess he moved out over that picture The Shade Room posted on Christmas, the one of T-Walk hugging Alexus."

"I know what picture it was," Rell said, and how could he *not* know? Tamera was in the picture, as well as her sister, Tirzah, and Bubbles. She talked about it at least once an hour. That photo had brought the number of Tamera's Instagram followers up from less than a thousand to more than three hundred thousand.

"They say Alexus and Bulletface are going to marriage counseling. I'm praying it works out. They have two kids together, you know?" Tamera was speaking as if she and Rell hadn't participated in a threesome with Queen A less than a week ago. "Not to mention the fact that they're the most powerful couple in the industry. Do you have any idea how many people are praying for their downfall? They shouldn't let that one little picture break up their marriage."

"He would *definitely* divorce her ass if he knew I had my dick in her that night at the concert," Rell said, pitching his half-smoked Newport out the window. He had his Glock 23 pistol on his lap; the Tec-9 was in his wife's Louis Vuitton shoulder bag on the back seat. There was a 16-shot magazine in the Glock and a 30-round extended magazine in the belly pocket of his hoodie.

Tamera looked at the Glock disapprovingly. "Uhh, we're out of Chicago now. You can put that gun away. And I hope you enjoyed that threesome, because it'll never happen again."

"Don't kill my dreams. Let's meet Rihanna first."

"Rihanna just unfollowed J-Lo for posting a pic with Drake."

"Ha!" Rell laughed and shook his head, tucking the gun into his waistline.

"I know, right? I died." Tamera checked her phone. They were actually in Michigan City now, pulling into a Meijer gas station. Beyond the gas station was a Meijer supermarket. "We're three minutes from Southgate Apartments now. We'll gas up and drive over there to find the truck. Shit, we stick out like a sore thumb in this Benz. We should've came in the Escalade."

She was right. Both the gas station and the supermarket's parking lot were packed with pickup trucks and cars, most American and most at least five years old. Several pairs of eyes turned to the flawless white Mercedes Benz S550 as Tamera pulled up to a pump. A short fat black man in a dirty gray jacket and skullcap who was pumping gas into an early nineties model Cadillac in front of them stared right in at them with inquisitive eyes, undoubtedly wondering who they were and how they were able to afford such a vehicle as the one they were sitting in.

"I didn't bring any cash," Tamera said, putting the car in park and turning to Rell. "Give me two twenties. You want anything?"

Rell reached into the right-hand pocket of his sweatpants and dragged out a rubber-banded fold of cash that was all of six inches thick. There were three separated denominations of band-new dollars in the bankroll: hundreds, fifties, and twenties. He unbanded the twenties and gave Tamera four of them.

"Newport 100's," he said, re-pocketing the cash, "blunt wraps, big bag of Cool Ranch Doritos, twenty-ounce Pepsi, and some peanut M&M's. Matter fact, get two of each."

"Wouldn't it be messed up if Bulletface really did find out about what Alexus did with us backstage at the concert?" Tamera said thoughtfully, because that was the way her brain worked. She was always going back to previous topics of conversation that Rell had commenced and treating them as if they were her own ideas. "That would make you the male version of Becky with the good hair."

"You gon' be Tamera with the black eye if you don't go and get my chips," Rell said, and pushed open his door.

He stepped out, his hoodie and sweatpants rippling around him in the keen breeze, and started around to the gas tank. "Put thirty-five on pump two, baby," he said to Tamera as she headed into the gas station. She offered him a middle finger to let him know she'd heard. He chuckled twice, shook his head, and turned his attention to the surrounding area.

The fat man was no longer studying the Benz. He was still gassing up his Caddy, but now he was gazing at something on his smartphone, as stone-faced as a Buckingham Palace sentinel. At pump four, there was a slender black girl of good height in denim jeans, sneakers, and an ugly Christmas sweater that didn't look so ugly on her. Her vehicle was a maroon Buick Regal, and while she stood at the pump, a shorter girl of the same medium-brown complexion leaned back against the passenger door. The two girls – sister, by the looks of them – were surreptitiously observing Rell, using quick, furtive glances instead of blatant stares. They chatted back and forth with pretty smiles on their pretty faces.

Rell wanted another cigarette, but he knew better than to smoke around fuel islands. The sun glittered on his back windshield and he squinted. It was forty-three degrees in both Michigan City and Chicago today, if the weather info on Tamera's iPhone was to be believed. Not exactly warm, but much more desirable than the below zero temps of days prior.

He switched the pump to "on" and pulled out the nozzle, then unscrewed the gas cap and began to pump fuel.

"Hey! Boy with the Benz!" It was the shorter girl.

Rell looked up and gave her a grin and a wave.

"Where you from?" she asked.

"Chicago," Rell said.

The girl and her taller comrade both smiled. "Was that your girlfriend who just went in the gas station?" the short girl asked.

"Something like that. Why?"

"Just asking. We ain't never seen y'all around, that's all. How long y'all been in M.C.?"

"About two minutes."

"Y'all got family out here?"

"Who are you and why are you asking me all these questions?"

The short girl laughed. "Oh, my bad. I'm Keyanna, with a K, and this is my sister, Krystal, also with a K. We're from Flint, but we moved her when they tried to kill us with the water. We live in Southgate Apartments, like right up the road from here."

Rell could almost feel a lightbulb appearing over his head, like in an old *Tom and Jerry* cartoon. His eyes lit up. His cordial grin grew into an inspirational smile.

"We're actually, uhh," he said, ruminating hard, "thinking about moving here. We're just here to look around and learn the town today. Shit, we don't know a soul out here. You mind if we come and chill with y'all?"

Keyanna raised her eyebrows and turned to her sister, who immediately nodded and said, "Sure. I mean, I'm about to go to work at six, but you're welcome to come over. Like she told you, we're not from here, either. We only know a couple of people here. Basically just our neighbors and the people we work with. I don't mind if you and your girl come over and kick it with us."

Just then, Tamera came strolling out of the gas station. Her smart eyes flicked from Rell to the two pretty girls and back to Rell again. She was carrying a tan plastic bag full of goodies.

Don't fuck this up, Rell thought with a nervous smile. He decided it was best to give it all to Tamera now to keep her from going off.

"Baby, that's Keyanna, and that's her sister Krystal," he said, pointing as he made the formal introductions. "I let them know we were here to learn our way around town before we find a place to live, and they invited us to kick it with them for a while. They live in Southgate Apartments. She said it's right up the road from here."

The light turned on in Tamera's eyes, and a wave of relief flooded Rell's chest. It was a good thing he'd married such a quick-witted woman. She was almost always on the same page with him.

Tamera gave the girls a wave and said, "You two are truly a blessing. I thought I was going to spend the rest of my day with nobody but this crazy man to talk to."

"It's cool," Krystal said, and Rell thought she bore a striking resemblance to Keri Hilson. "Y'all can just follow us to my apartment."

"Sounds like a plan," Tamera said cheerfully.

Rell returned the nozzle to the pump, got back in the passenger's seat, and smiled at Tamera as she pulled off behind the girls in the Buick. She smiled, too, feeling his smiling eyes boring into the side of her face.

"Tell me you love me," he said.

"Shut up."

"I'm the man, ain't I?"

"You ain't shit." Tamera chuckled.

Rell lowered the overhead visor and admired his handsome reflection. He was good-looking and he knew it, his knowing of the functional and non-arrogant sort. Only now he was playing arrogant to get under Tamera's skin.

"When you look this good," he said, "things just seem to work out for you. You know what I mean?" he licked his lips, stroked his goatee. "Now we can just kick back, wait for the sun to go down, make our exit, and then get the job done."

"You are so extra," Tamera remarked.

"Extra handsome."

"Extra annoying."

"Haters, haters. Haters everywhere I go. Haters everywhere I look. Haters everywhere." Laughing, he leaned toward Tamera to kiss her on the cheek. He half-expected her to shun the peck, but she took it like a champ. It was a loud smack of a kiss that made her smile widen an inch or two.

"Did you give them our names?" Tamera asked.

"Of course not."

"Good. I'm...Tonya."

"And I'm..." Rell hesitated, lighting another Newport. "Drell. Nah, nah, nah. Fuck that. *Drill*. Yeah, that's it. I'm Drill, 'cause that's exactly what the fuck it's gon' be when I catch the nigga who shot my brother."

Chapter 5

Bubbles sauntered into GAM's, automatically sweeping an eye about for who was there and where they were seated. Great Aunt Micki herself was way in the back of the restaurant, standing at a customer's table. She gestured and Rob, the headwaiter, seated Bubbles and Juice at a favored table up front.

They had arrived in a chauffeured black Mercedes Maybach 62-S. As Bubbles slipped out of her full-length Russian sable fur coat, she couldn't help thinking about how royal she'd felt stepping out of the Maybach. She was already considered somewhat of a celebrity, thanks to her past relations with billionaire rap superstar Bulletface, but emerging from the sleek black luxury car, she had felt like a *queen*. The feeling was still surging through her as she cast her eyes around the exclusive restaurant again, taking in the important faces. There were ball players, corporate execs, and even a few members of the cast of *Empire*. GAM's was always chock-full of celebrities, a five-star black-owned restaurant and lounge where the who's who of the black community came to dine and mingle.

Juice ordered a double Hennessy on the rocks, and Bubbles ordered a large bottle of vitamin water.

"We'll order food when our guests arrive," Juice said, waving the waiter away. He was seated across the table from Bubbles, smiling.

Bubbles shot a glance at the two empty chairs, one on her right, the other on Juice's left. As bad as she wanted to question him about the unnamed dinner guests, she couldn't risk spoiling this magical moment.

"Why are you so good to me?" Bubbles asked softly, and she wasn't asking for the sake of romance. It was a question she really wanted answered.

Why wouldn't I be?" Juice said. The smile was still there, but he was serious now – as serious as he could be in this lively atmosphere, anyway. "I mean, you're Bubbles. You're Lakita Thomas. You're beautiful, you're intelligent, you're loyal, and you made me a lot better than I was before we got together. That's four good reasons right there, and I ain't even got to all that ass you got yet."

"I can't stand you." She shook her head, beaming.

"No, but for real. You're an amazing woman. I'm lucky to have you. After me and my ex-wife called it quits and my son got killed, I stopped giving a fuck about everything. It was like I was in a trance. All I did was buy a few bricks, get rid of 'em and re-up, buy a few more bricks, get rid of 'em, and re-up. Over and over and over again, that's all I did. Then I would sit in the house, smoking blunts and cigarettes, drinking beer and this good shit here." He held up his glass and fixed his gaze on the clean brown liquid inside it.

"Then Myesha came over to my house to get her hair done by the twins," he went on, lowering his glass and shifting his eyes back to her, "and you came with her. The moment you walked in that door was the moment I started giving a fuck again. I remember it like it was yesterday. I still remember how good you smelled when you walked over and gave me a hug by the kitchen sink."

"And I remember how bad you smelled," Bubbles countered with her wiseass grin on full display.

Juice loosed a jovial chuckle and took a swig of his cognac. "I ran right up those stairs and took a shower, though."

"You did, you did. I'll give you that much. Came back looking and smelling real nice. I remember the whole outfit."

"Then we sat on the couch and smoked some loud."

"Mm-hmm." Bubbles nodded. "Then we went upstairs to watch *Narcos* on Netflix, and those two boys kicked in your back door and robbed you. I had to shoot that boy in the face with that shotgun." She trembled at the memory, which seemed to play in ultra-high definition in her mind every time she thought about it. "Jesus Christ, Juice. That was the craziest day of my life."

"It was the best day of mine. I might've lost over a hundred thousand dollars, but I gained you. Can't put a price on that. Shit, look at us now. Started from the bottom, now we're here." He snatched a quick glance at his own gold Rolex wrist-watch. "It's three o'clock now. Our guests should be pulling up any minute."

His expressive brown eyes were fixed on Bubbles – the woman of his dreams, let him tell it. Bubbles wanted to believe in his love, but she was well aware of what had drawn him to her from the very start. She was a big-bootied black woman with a cute face and a small waist, a former stripper who had once bounced her ass for cash to keep her finances in order. Just about every black man she knew wanted to be with her, but they wanted her for all the wrong reasons. Juice had wanted her for her physical appearance. She worried that one day he would grow tired of her and move on to another bad bitch with a big butt.

Revel in the moment, she thought to herself, and forced a grateful smile.

"I wish I could read your thoughts," Juice said, leaning forward. "I can tell when you're really thinking about something, just not what it is."

"What are you talking about?"

"You know what I'm talking about. Just a second ago. The look you had in your eyes."

"You're seeing things."

"What's up with all those paintings you got in your basement? You plan on selling any of 'em?"

A burst of excited air ballooned her lungs. The excitement's sudden arrival filled her like cotton in a stuffed animal. She found herself on the verge of shouting out about her artwork, and she bit the urge back desperately.

There was an art studio in the basement of her Lake Forest home. It was where she spent the majority of her free time these days. Ever since grade school, she had been a talented artist with a keen eye for detail, and her knack for drawing on things had not at all faded in the years since. She considered it her hidden talent. She could make her ass clap and bounce with the best of them, but were there any other strippers out there who could actually paint something worth looking at? She didn't think there were.

If asked to name her favorite piece of work, she likely would have looked blank. If pressed, she might have said it was the painting of Donald Trump reaching down into a box full of kittens with a cold glint of malice in his eyes, but even that would have been a lie, something told just to make the question go away. In truth, she wasn't the kind of artist who had (or even needed to have) favorites. She simply loved to paint.

"No," Bubbles said, after a moment, "I don't intend on selling any of them. I just paint to paint. It's more of a hobby than anything. Don't get me wrong – I *love* painting, but it's not something I'm looking to make a career out of."

"Well, I think you should. You're really good at it," Juice said.

By now nearly all the tables were taken, and there were even a few people standing at the back of the restaurant near the bar. Conversation, animated and jittery, zinged and caromed around the high-ceilinged red room like bowling pins after a hand strike.

Juice snatched another quick glance at his watch and gazed at Bubbles with starry absorption. She touched her face and found it was eerily warm. She lowered the tips of her fingers to her carotid artery and felt her pulse – it was racing. It wasn't the excitement of her artwork now; that intense feeling had faded, at least temporarily. No, it was something else, something about the mysterious double-date.

"Max Farmer!" a kindred spirit shouted from the back of the restaurant, and there was spontaneous applause and chatter.

Bubbles was seated with her back to the restaurant's front entrance. She twisted around in her chair, looked at the young black couple that had just entered, and immediately sprung from her chair and rushed toward them.

Max Farmer was the Florida-born star running back of the Atlanta Falcons, but it was his date who had Bubbles up and running as if *she* was the running back.

It was the bad-ass yellow bone stripper who'd been one of Atlanta's most talked-about exotic dancers for several years now. Her name was Tasia Olsen, but everybody called her Baddie Barbie, or just Baddie or Barbie for short. She and Bubbles had both garnered a deluge of negative press last year for their love triangle with then newly-married hip-hop mogul Bulletface, during which time they had established an unbreakable bond of friendship that Bubbles deeply cherished.

"Bitch!" Barbie said in an excited whisper as Bubbles wrapped her up in a snug, swiveling hug. "Girl, I missed your crazy ass."

"I missed you too." Bubbles drew back, teary-eyed, and smiled. "Why didn't you tell me you were coming?" She gave Max a one-armed hug of unimportance and let him go on to shake hands with Juice.

Not surprisingly, Barbie was slaying in a flowing red fur, open to reveal the matching Givenchy shirt and black jeans she wore beneath it. Her hair was dyed as red as the coat, impeccable curls that framed her perfect yellowish brown face and betrayed her ruthless personality.

"I wanted to pop up on your ass," Barbie said, her voice a step above a whisper. "I saw you tag your man in a pic on the Gram, so I hit him in the DM and set it up. But listen: I wanna know if you've been getting the same phone calls I've been getting."

"Phone calls?" Bubbles knitted her brow. "What kind of phone calls?"

"Blake hasn't called you?"

"No."

"Well, he's been calling me ever since Christmas – the day him and Alexus split – talking about how much he misses being with us, that he's sorry about all the crazy shit we had to go through."

"He's *sorry*?"

"I know, right? That's what I'm saying. His wife sent the fucking Mexican Mafia at me. Motherfuckers tried to shoot me in the bathroom at Lenox Square Mall, then again right after me and my sister Fantasia made it home. She got hit in the shoulder, and I ended up in the witness protection program. I'm not about to put myself through that again."

"Who are you telling? They kidnapped me from my own house, hung me by my ankles in an abandoned warehouse, and threatened to cut me open with a damn chainsaw." Bubbles shook her head emphatically. "Damn, that. He knows better than to call me. I'm happy with the man I got."

"I'm feeling the same way. You know why I was fucking with him from the jump. I just wanted to know who killed my sister."

"Jantasia, right?"

"Mm-hmm. It was three of us. Jantasia, Fantasia, and me. With all the shit Alexus sent my way, I wouldn't be a bit surprised if it was really her who killed my sister. But forget all that. Let's eat so we can go out and get our party on. It's been a long while since I last visited Chicago." Tasia "Baddie Barbie" Olsen was turning to venture toward their table when she twisted her neck to look at Bubbles again. "Oh. Shit. I almost forgot to tell you. I got mad at Blake the last time he called my phone this morning. I told him he needed to be calling his nasty-ass wife and asking her about the threesome she had with some married couple backstage at the Deja and D-Boy concert in Los Angeles last week."

Bubbles gasped. "I told you to keep that between us!" She said, a morsel of panic coloring her voice. "That wasn't supposed to get out!"

"I told you I was mad," Tasia explained. "I just wanted the nigga to leave me alone. It worked. His ass stopped calling."

They walked to the table and sat down. The four of them chatted idly as they selected from the menu and ate their main courses, sides, and desserts. All the while, Bubbles thought about the secret Barbie had revealed to Blake, wondering if it would in any way damage Juice's business relationship with Blake – or perhaps land Tamera and Rell in a world of trouble.

Chapter 6

The two billionaires seated on the white Italian leather sofa across from Dr. Melonie Farr's desk were both sitting with their arms crossed over their chests and their faces set in stone. They were on opposite ends of the sofa. It was 3:35 p.m. The session had begun five minutes ago, and so far it had been nothing but silence. Three hundred seconds and counting.

They were in Dr. Farr's office in West Hollywood, the place where just about every A-list celebrity in Hollywood came to vent when they were grieving the loss of a loved one, or battling depression, or struggling to cope with the many burdens that came with being filthy rich in an industry full of drug addicts and sex fiends, or fighting with their unashamedly cheating spouses over suspected infidelities.

The latter "or" was what had the silent billionaire couple sitting in Dr. Farr's office on this beautiful eighty-degree winter afternoon in West Hollywood. Farr's exorbitant fee of $1,000-an-hour was certainly a raindrop in the Pacific to this particular couple — *Forbes* had the wife's net worth listed as $82 billion, and the husband's as $1.7 billion — but allowing the deathly quiet to continue would not be beneficial to either of them.

"Alexus?" Farr said

"This insecure-ass nigga," Alexus Costilla-King snapped, thrusting a thumb in her husband's direction, "has the nerve to get mad at me because of some picture somebody took of me giving the shortest hug in world history to my ex."

"Ain't *shit* insecure about me," Blake King said through his tightly clenched, diamond-encrusted platinum teeth. "This dumb bitch just can't keep her legs closed. That's the real problem."

"I got your bitch," Alexus said, scowling fiercely at him.

Dr. Farr raised a brown hand, pink palm out. "One at a time, please. I'd also appreciate it if we could cut out the foul language."

"He's looking for another reason to start cheating on me again," Alexus said acidly. "That's all this is. He's fucked so many bitches since we've been together. *So* many." She began to count off the alleged mistresses on her fingers. "That stripper bitch they call Bubbles – the bitch *he* took a picture with last week, but we won't get into that – the Barbie bitch, Maliah, Tahiry, Rihanna, Cereniti…Lord knows how many other bitches he done fucked. Oh, let's not forget about Nona, and that bitch Janautica…who would've *killed* his stupid ass if I hadn't saved him. I'm all out of fingers now, and I'm just getting started."

Alexus sat back – *threw* herself back – and folded her arms tightly over her chest again. She thrust her bottom lip out, flared her nostrils, and gritted her teeth. Dr. Farr could see the jaw muscles working overtime. Alexus was by far the most stunningly attractive woman Farr had ever known. A lot of people considered Alexus to be Nicki Minaj's long-lost twin, but Farr thought the wealthy young black-and-Mexican bombshell fell more in line with *Orange is the New Black's* Dascha Palanco. She had on a skintight long-sleeved sequined minidress that was as white as the high-heeled Louboutins on her feet. The mini shimmered like the large white diamonds that encircled her neck and wrists. Her long straight black hair was parted down the middle. Her vivid green eyes were stringent slits.

In a blink, Dr. Farr ticked her eyes over to Blake King. It was as if he had just emerged from the machine that had transformed the scrawny kid in that *Captain America* movie into the muscled-up superhero. He had tattoos all over his arms and on his neck, and teardrops inked on his handsome dark face. His black V-neck T-shirt clung to him like a second skin, showing off his powerful musculature. He wore black Balmain jeans and black-and-red Jordan sneakers. Four plain white diamond necklaces gleamed on his chest, and an icy Hublot watch was clasped to his left wrist. He was a gangster-rapper, albeit a sexy one, and there were nights when Farr pleasured herself with him in mind before going to bed. How anyone could ever cheat on a man as fine as Blake was beyond Dr. Farr's comprehension.

"That's old shit," Blake said. "I ain't fucked nobody but her crazy ass ever since we got back together last year. It's her who's the thot."

Alexus offered him a middle finger without looking at him. "Like I said, he's insecure. You can ask everybody who was in that restaurant with me. I was crying over this insecure-ass man when T-Walk came in. He touched my shoulder, I hugged him for one itty-bitty ass second, and I don't know who snapped the picture, but I'd bet my life it was somebody who wanted to see me and Blake break up. Hell, it might've been T-Walk who set it up. Whatever the case, one lousy picture shouldn't be the straw that broke the camel's back. Especially not when I put up with all the bitches he's been with. If that's all it took for this bitch nigga to leave, then he didn't wanna be with me in the first place."

"Stop calling me out my name," Blake growled, staring right at Alexus. His diamond-encrusted platinum teeth were clenched again. His beastly snarl peeled his lips back and exposed those expensive biters.

Alexus turned to him, clearly unmoved by his threatening demeanor. "Bitch-nigga, bitch-nigga, bitch-nigga." Her head arced from side to side with every syllable, and she clapped her hands in front of her. Not the sort of ratchet gesticulations you might expect from a woman who could spend a million dollars every day for the rest of her life and still have a massive fortune leftover, but Alexus was not your ordinary billionaire. She lived a life of luxury, but deep down, she was still just a hood chick from Texas. Combine that hood girl with her former role as the top boss of her paternal family's Mexican drug cartel, and you got one hell of a fearless woman.

"Alexus," Dr. Farr said firmly. "Let's not antagonize. We're trying to get this marital issue resolved. I can't do it alone. Now I want you two to look at each other and listen to the questions I'm about to ask."

Nodding his head, Blake stood up and turned to face his wife, giving Farr his profile. He was a tall man, about six feet two inches from scalp to heel. His muscles were large rolling slabs under his skin. His iPhone looked very puny clutched in one of his huge fists. Alexus got up quicker than he had, and they stared each other down like two boxers preparing to touch gloves and duke it out.

"I didn't suggest standing," Farr said, "but I guess it'll work." She scooted forward in her swivel chair and laced her fingers together on her desk. "Alexus, do you reme——"

"I just wanna see my kids every weekend," Blake said, cutting Farr off in a hurry. "That's all I want. I'm not trying to get back with you, I'm not trying to work nothing out. I'm not trying to do nothing but see my kids."

Alexus began to cry with a mean face. "I fucking *made* you!" she exclaimed, her fists balled up at her sides. "And you're going to leave *me*? Over *nothing*?" Her face was turning red. Now she was the most stunningly attractive *angry* woman Farr had ever seen.

"I ain't even mad about the picture. Fuck that picture. You fucked a nigga last week."

"I fucked a nigga last week?"

"Bitch, you know you fucked a nigga at that concert! What, you thought I wouldn't find out?"

There was a coffee mug full of green tea on Farr's desk. *WORLD'S GREATEST SHRINK*, the mug proclaimed. Farr picked it up and took a sip.

"You need to check your sources," Alexus said. "The only concert I've been to this month was the D-Boy and Deja concert, and I'd really like to know how I could have cheated on you when I was there if I was with you from the time I got there until the time we went home. See, *that's* the problem. You're listening to everybody *but* your wife. It's supposed to be us against the world, but you switched over to the world's side. Now it's me against everybody. You're working with the enemy, Blake. You're giving them exactly what they want, and you're too blind to see it."

"So I'm supposed to believe you didn't do anything with Rell and his wife?"

"Are you fucking retarded?"

Blake looked at Alexus. She looked back for some time.

"You *are* fucking retarded." She said this in tones of amazement.

"Stop disrespecting me."

"I call it like I see it." Alexus put her hands on her hips. "You're listening to people who don't want to see us together. That's retarded."

"I ain't listened to nobody," Blake said, but he didn't sound too convincing.

Alexus pointed to the iPhone in his fist. "Get her on the phone," she said. "That's what I want you to do. Whoever the bitch is that told you I fucked Rell – and I know it's a female; ain't no man said no shit like that – get the bitch on the phone. I wanna hear this lie myself. It had to be a good-ass lie for you to believe it when you know for a fact that I left my restaurant and went straight to the concert with you. Especially since the nigga I supposedly fucked was with you the whole time that I wasn't with you. Come on now. You can't possibly be that slow."

A small smile made a crescent of Dr. Farr's mouth. "Blake?"

He turned to Dr. Farr.

"Is it true that you were socializing with the guy the night this allegedly occurred?" Farr asked carefully.

"Sure it is," Alexus answered for him, her eyes flashing with sardonic brilliance. "I can show you the video on YouTube. Just search 'D-Boy and Deja Staples Center concert,' and you'll see Rell on the stage with him. I didn't even get to meet that man. I had his wife and her sister out to dinner with me. That's the only reason I even know Rell's name."

Looking defeated, Blake sat down on the sofa. Alexus smiled a triumphant smile and plopped down onto his lap. She hugged his head to her bosom and gave the crisp waves of his short hair a rub.

"This is the Blake and Alexus I like to see," Dr. Farr said, nodding, smiling, and lifting her glass mug of tea. She sipped. "You can't allow this great thing of yours to be poisoned by the words of gossip mongers. You're the most powerful black couple in the industry. Tabloids are already raking in millions of dollars for putting the news of your breakup on their front covers, all because Blake was spotted in New York without you by his side."

"I've been telling him that," Alexus said, and kissed him on the cheek.

"Yeah, a'ight," Blake said. "Take another picture with T-Walk and see what happens. And I'm calling Juice to get Rell's number."

"See how retarded this fool is?" Alexus said incredulously. "He was literally right next to the guy that whole night, yet he still believes some bitch over me. Is that crazy or is that crazy?"

"Who can you two trust if you can't even trust each other?" Dr. Farr knew her opinion on the matter was biasedly one-sided, but she couldn't help it. She was the most sought after psychiatrist in the country because of her close friendship with Alexus. In her eyes, Queen A could do no wrong.

"He still ain't told us who told him that lie," Alexus said. She slipped off his lap and sat next to him. "I need to know who said it. Obviously that bitch's word carries more weight than mine does."

"Are you two back together now?" Farr asked.

"For now," Blake said immediately. And the words poured out as if a cork had been pulled from the bottom of his soul. "See, the shit between me, her and T-Walk is way deeper than that picture. Around the time I first made it big, rapping, I used a home security app I had on my phone to check and see what she was doing in our house while I was on the road. I caught her sucking T-Walk's dick. Saw it with my own eyes."

Alexus sighed. "But *I'm* the one bringing up old shit," she muttered.

"Plus," Blake sailed on, "he's the reason I got these scars on my face and all over my body. He sent some niggas to kill me right in front of my mama's houses. My mama had to see me full of holes on Christmas Eve. That ain't the kind of shit you can just let go. When I first found out the nigga was alive, I tried to let the shit go. But that picture – I think he did that on purpose. You gotta know T-Walk to know what I'm talking about. I mean, don't get me wrong, he's a real nigga. But he loves Alexus, almost to the point of obsession. He went to war with me over Alexus. Not drugs, not territory, not money I owed him. It was all over Alexus. And she didn't make it any better, fucking him and fucking me and fucking him and fucking me. She fueled the fire. Fanned the flames. And she *knows* that shit."

He pushed the tip of his forefinger into her cheek for emphasis, and in his wife's eyes, Dr. Farr saw the guilt of a thousand adulterers. Farr recalled the days of T-Walk and Alexus quite vividly. Trintino Walkson was yet another ridiculously fine specimen of man, a light-completed paragon of handsome who was hardly ever seen out without a finely-tailored three-piece suit clinging to his tall figure. The critics had a lot to say about Alexus, but now one of them could say she had bad taste in men.

"All that's in the past," Dr. Farr said, sipping again. "T-Walk is with that reality show girl now, and you and Alexus have been going strong for a while. If T-Walk is able to get either of you to abandon the other, there would have to be a weakness there to begin with. Work it as hard and unbreakable as steel. Because as she just said a moment ago, it truly is you and her against the world."

The Brick Man 5

Chapter 7

"I seeee...four...and a possible," Rell said, carefully studying his playing cards with an unlit Newport stuck between the middle knuckles of his first and second fingers.

They were seated around a square blue table in the cramped dining room area of Krystal's two-bedroom apartment. Tamera was seated across from Rell, his partner in the game of Spades the four of them were playing. She was the only one without a bottle of Corona beer in front of her. Her beverage of choice was a can of Red Bull. Overhead, a ceiling fan with dust-laden wooden blades spun round and round in a big slow circle. There was a computer on a desk behind Rell's chair, and Young M.A.'s "Ooouuu" was blaring from its speakers.

"Let's pause this game for a minute," Keyanna said, and placed her thirteen cards face-down on the table. "We need some Molly, some powder, or some weed. I can't just drink beer and smoke cigarettes."

Tamera's eyes widened and her eyebrows lifted.

Rell uttered a brief, humorless sound that was like a low growl. "You're serious, ain't you?" he said.

"What's wrong with I' high?" Keyanna said. "Y'all don't smoke weed?"

"Ain't nothing wrong with it," Tamera said in a high-flung tone that said there was something wrong with it. "We smoke weed all the time, though. Just never tried the other stuff. At least I haven't. I don't know about Drill over there." She flicked her eyes in his direction, smiled with one side of her mouth, and turned back to the short redbone girl. "We did want some weed. Not no bullshit-ass loud, either. Loud pack or no pack."

"Yeah," Rell said, putting his cards down in a neat stack and picking up his lighter, "who got that loud?"

"Lil Phil got that sack," Krystal said. "He got everything: Molly, loud, powder, hard, Xanax bars, Percs. He lives in one of the buildings up front."

51

"I can run over there," Keyanna volunteered. "I got about thirty bucks. He'll give me a good deal. Him and his brother have been tryna get with me ever since we met at the gas station."

Krystal laughed briefly. "And no, we don't be posted up at the gas station looking for friends."

"Could've fooled me." Rell grinned, turning up his beer.

Keyanna started to get up, but Krystal waved for her to sit down.

"Lil Phil ain't home," Krystal said. "His car wasn't out there when we pulled in. We gotta hit his phone."

Rell pretty much had Southgate Apartments all figured out. The redbrick buildings were bunched together, creating rectangular parking lots ("courts") that were outlined with sidewalks. The sidewalks ran around to the rear of the buildings where there were one bedroom apartments. There was a small park for children at the back of the apartment complex. Rell had taken the time to study the complex's geography on Tamera's phone during the trip here, so it was easy for him to get the full grasp of its layout as she'd driven into the front entrance.

His eyes had been everywhere at once, noting, cataloguing, starring, searching. He'd counted eight pickup trucks; three of them were black, and none of them were Dodge Rams. But with the sheer number of vehicles jammed into the parking spaces, there were bound to be trucks he'd missed.

"You know Phil always leaves his brother with some bags to sell," Keyanna said, clearly fiending for that high.

But Krystal was already dialing a number on her Samsung smartphone, holding up a forefinger that basically told her shorter sibling to wait one minute. They both had long, straight black hair, scooped back in modest ponytails. Krystal had discarded the jolly sweater upon entering the apartment. Now she wore a long-sleeve shirt over her form-fitting jeans. Rell had always been attracted to dark-skinned women, and if not for his marriage to Tamera, he knew for certain that he would be all over Krystal.

He pried his eyes away from Krystal and turned to her sister. "So," he asked, puffing his cigarette and gazing at Keyanna through a haze of rising smoke, "what's the hustle like out here?"

"Same as everywhere else. Niggas tryna eat, cops tryna lock 'em up and throw away the key. Only difference is we had a lot of big-money niggas n Flint. They don't have as many out here, but it's the same story. You got some real hustlers and you got some broke-ass wanna-be hustlers. You got some real get-money bitches and you got the broke bum bitches that sit around and hate all day."

"What about the cake prices?"

"I don't really know a whole lot about that. You'd have to ask Lil Phil. All I know is he paid something like ten grand for a nine-piece a few weeks ago. He got it from a Latin King in East Chicago." She said all this in low tones, more than likely because her sister was on the phone with the guy whose business she was openly discussing.

"*East* Chicago?" Rell frowned quizzically. "You mean the eastside of Chicago?"

"No. I mean East Chicago. It's here in Indiana, by Gary and Hammond."

"Never heard of it."

"Well, you'll know all about Indiana soon enough. Trust me, these hoes out here see you and your girl pushing that clean-ass Benz, they'll be tryna fuck you while at the same time tryna be her best friend."

Tamera and Rell looked at each other, and something passed between them, some perfectly silent communication from which Keyanna was excluded. Tamera's eyes seemed to threaten the lives of all those hoes who would be tryna fuck Rell while at the same time tryna be her best friend. The corners of her mouth lifted into a smirk that was as cold as the sweating Corona in Rell's left hand.

"Drill," Krystal said, "how much you looking to get?"

Rell turned to Krystal. "I got fifty," he said.

"A fifty of the loud," she said into the phone. "And me and Key got twenty for Miss Molly. She said show her some love, too. Okay, just text me when you pull up...yup, one." She ended the call. "He's at the L right now. Said he'll be pulling up in ten minutes. He was coming over to drink with us anyway."

"Yeah right," Keyanna said with a suck of the teeth and a roll of the eyes. "He wasn't coming over here until you told him we had some money for his ass."

Rell said, "Tell him to grab a fifth of Henny. I'll pay him soon as he get here."

While Krystal typed the text message, Keyanna looked at Rell and asked, "What do you do for a living? Because I know money when I see it."

"What makes you think I got some money?"

"That hoodie and those sweatpants say Moncler on the strings, and the whole fit is brand-new. That's at least two thousand dollars alone. At *least*. You got a gold Roley on your wrist, and it ain't ticking, so it ain't fake. You got on Christian Louboutin kicks and your girl got on Louboutin heels. You look like you just left the barber shop and she looks like she just walked out the salon. She got this big-ass ring on her finger. Y'all got that Benz. I might not be the smartest bitch in Southgate, but I know enough to know when I'm sitting at the table with a nigga who *really* got that bag."

Rell shook his head. "I ain't got no money," he said, grinning. He pointed at Tamera. "My sugar-mama over there – she's the rich one."

"You know that's a lie," Tamera said, and smiled.

Krystal put her phone back down on the table. "He's bringing it," she said laconically, smiling into Rell's eyes for a fleeting moment. When she did that, he could see – for the first time, really – that she was sexy as well as pretty. And she wasn't much of a talker.

Keyanna's eyes were on Tamera's ring. "How many carats is that?"

"Nine," Tamera said truthfully. "It belonged to his dad's wife before she passed away."

It looked like Keyanna was fixing her mouth to say something like "Awww, that's so *sweet*!" but she didn't get it out.

"*Oh my God*!" Krystal shouted shocking Rell all the way down to his shoes. She was gawking at Tamera. "You're the girl from the picture! The girl from the picture with Alexus! It's really you! Shit, Key, it's the girl who was in the picture with Queen fucking A!"

54

"It *is* her!" Keyanna said in utter disbelief. "She was in the pic with Bulletface too! We have one of Queen A's friends in our apartment!"

Both Krystal and Keyanna were on their feet now, staring at Tamera with wide eyes. Keyanna was fanning her face with her hands, as if she had suddenly become hot. Krystal's eyes were darting back and forth from the phone in her hand to Tamera's face, and Rell knew she was thumbing her way to one of those incriminating photos. There were three of them: one of Tamera, Tirzah, and Bubbles posing with Bulletface in front of the Sassafras Saloon in Hollywood last week; a second photo Alexus had snapped and posted for all 120 million of her Instagram followers to see; and a third of Tamera, Tirzah and Bubbles seated at the same table as Alexus stood hugging T-Walk. Three photos that had made Tamera and Tirzah internet famous overnight.

Rell sat there trying to come up with a way to regain control of the situation, and it was like trying to get a big sofa up a narrow flight of stairs. He was here to murder the man who'd shot his brother five times, and now two random girls knew his wife's identity. How could this have happened? It didn't seem like a mistake. It seemed like some fucked-up destiny. He looked from Krystal to Keyanna with his disbelieving eyes, which were watering from the Newport pasted in the middle of his mouth.

"I am not one of Queen A's friends," Tamera said with a nervous chuckle.

"And I'm not Keyanna Cartwright," Keyanna Cartwright said. "I can't believe it. I just cannot believe it. I'm actually standing here looking at somebody who knows Alexus Costilla. No wonder y'all pulled up in that clean-ass Benz. Shit. Un-fucking-believable."

"And you're Tamera, not Tonya," Krystal said, looking at her phone. "I'm on your page now. You're Tamera Lynn-Owens, and he's Rell."

"How in the hell did you just find my page?" Tamera asked.

"I've been following Bubbles since she was fucking with Bulletface. She has the same pic he posted of y'all on her page, but she tagged you in hers. See?" She thrust out her phone for Tamera to see, then snatched it back. "I just tapped the tag. Took me right to your page."

Well, this backfired, Rell thought to himself as he smashed his cancer stick out in the glass ashtray. He watched Keyanna skitter around the table to her sister's side to view the Instagram photos, her big butt rocking from side to side as she went.

"Y'all do know," Keyanna said, "that Bulletface and T-Walk are from right here in Michigan City, right?"

Rell shook his head. He hadn't known that little fact.

"Yep," Keyanna went on, slipping her hands palm-out into the back pockets of her tight jeans, "and Alexus used to live here, too, over on 8th and Willard. That's actually where she met Blake. Oooh, Tamera, you look amazing in your wedding dress!"

"Thank you," Tamera said slowly and uneasily. She looked to Rell, as if seeking his approval, but he was just as immersed in the quicksand as she was.

"I get it now," Keyanna said. "Rell and Drill. Tamera and Tonya." She giggled and shook her head. "Y'all ain't slick. Not in the least. So, umm, what are y'all really out here for? Is it to spy on T-Walk or something? Because I find it mighty funny that y'all showed up on the same day T-Walk came to town."

Tamera raised her eyebrows. "T-Walk's in this city? *Today?*"

"Mm-hmm. I was just talking to Krystal about going to the club to see him tonight. It's at the club that used to be his. I think they said it was The Swagger or something like that when he owned it, but the new owners changed it to Manna's."

"You actually had dinner with Alexus," Krystal said.

"That's what I'm saying," Keyanna said. "Was it just to clear the air over her being mad about the picture Bulletface took with Bubbles?"

Tamera sealed her lips with an invisible zipper. "I'm not allowed to talk about anything that was said or done that night," she said.

"That's that Illuminati shit right there," Keyanna accused. "Girl, we gotta take a picture together before you leave. I might be able to sell that shit to TMZ or something."

That did it – Rell was not about to have any pictures of his wife floating around in the same city he had traveled to in search of a man he meant to kill. He stood up, sliding his folding chair back so hard it actually tipped over backward. Krystal and Keyanna glanced back at him, their brows knitted together.

"We ain't taking no pictures," he said tightly. "A'ight? No pictures. We didn't come here for no goddamn photo shoot."

"Well," Keyanna said, "excuuuse me." She was a very pretty girl, like her sister, though she looked as if it might take a two-digit number to express her IQ.

Rell picked up his chair and unfolded it back to its sitting position. "Sit down so we can talk like sane people and not like some Alexus groupies," he said, and sat down. "I don't even want people to know we're here, let alone see our faces on social media. We didn't come here for that. A'ight?"

"Then what did y'all come here for?" Krystal asked, lowering herself back to her chair. Her voice was soft again. She didn't seem the least bit offended by Rell's sudden outburst.

The same could not be said for Keyanna, who stood next to Krystal's chair with her hands gripping her hips and a cantankerous grimace scrunching her pretty face into a mask of malice. Rell got the impression that she was the kind of girl who reeled men in with her irresistible looks and then ran them off with her pouty, argumentative ways.

"To get *away* from social media," Tamera said, and Rell could almost see a cape billowing out behind her like a sail, her quick-thinking brain the source of her superhuman powers. "I have over three hundred thousand people following me on Instagram now, and about two hundred and ninety-nine thousand of them just started following me within the last five days. Everywhere we go I get hounded with questions about Bulletface and Alexus. There's nothing fun or enjoyable about that. People think I'm rich all of a sudden, and Chicago is *not* the place to be when people think you're rich. Have you seen the news lately? The Fed-Ex drivers keep getting robbed at gunpoint. They're carjacking everybody, doing all kinds of home invasions, killing people for nothing. It's chaos, and ever since those pictures went viral, people have been running up to me in the streets, at the mall, at the grocery store -everywhere. And I don't know if they're reaching for a phone or a gun."

"Awww." Krystal reached out and touched the back of Tamera's hand. "I see. Well, it ain't like that here. It's nothing like the big cities. They have, like, one or two murders a year here in M.C., if that. I hear it was really bad about five or six years ago, but that was when Blake and T-Walk's crews were going at it. It's calmed down a lot since then. The Feds snatched most of the big dope boys up, and the police cleaned up most of the troublemakers. There are a few groups of gangs sprinkled here and there, but nothing to worry about."

"All I want is some peace, some time away from everything," Tamera said, and were those tears gleaming along her lower eyelids? Yes, they were definitely tears. This stellar performance deserved an Oscar. "I'm sick and tired of people running up to me and taking my picture. I'm tired of being recognized. I just want to be *me*. That's it. That's all I want."

"I know," Krystal said, not knowing anything. "Let's just relax for a while. Forget this card game. Lil Phil's on the way over here with the drinks and the loud. You are about to loosen up and enjoy yourself tonight." She got up and went to Tamera's aid, wrapping her arms around Tamera's shoulders.

Two seconds later, someone knocked at the front door. It was a heavy knock, three big thumps, and beyond the door, Rell heard what sounded like two men laughing out loud about something. Keyanna answered the door and in walked a tall man in a leather Colts jacket. There was a second man on the porch who didn't come in, and Rell wondered if he might be a neighbor. Keyanna shut the door on the man on the porch and followed the first man into the living room.

"This is Lil Phil, y'all," she said, no longer looking mean in the face.

Lil Phil looked more like Uncle Phil from the *Fresh Prince of Bel-Air*. He was fat. His jacket was open, and his belly pushed his dark blue sweater out to a point where Rell half suspected he had

58

swallowed a beach ball. He had two plastic bags in one hand, two more in the other, and he was chewing on a toothpick. Coal-black and wide-faced, he looked right at Rell, then his eyes flicked over to Krystal.

"You didn't tell me y'all had company," Lil Phil said, putting the plastic bags down on the coffee-table.

"Didn't know I had to," Krystal said, still hugging Tamera.

The fat man grinned, rolled his toothpick from one corner of his mouth to the other, shrugged out of his jacket, and then pushed his Colts skullcap up a notch on his forehead.

"You better start," Lil Phil said jovially, plopping down on the living room sofa and leaning back to dig in the front pockets of his baggy jeans. "I mean, I am still the man of this house, right? Right, Krystal?" He grinned on endlessly, tossing two sandwich bags onto the table in front of him. One bag was full of white capsules, and there was weed in the second one.

Rell went and joined the fat man in the living room. He shook Uncle Phil's mammoth paw, introduced himself as Drill and his wife as Tonya, and took a spot on the loveseat. He dug out his thick mound of cash and was wriggling the twenties loose when he heard Tamera's cell phone ring. He knew it was her phone, because the ringtone was a Dreezy song, and Tamera was a die-hard fan of Dreezy's. Tamera brought him the phone.

"It's Juice," she said, handing it to him. "I know he ain't calling for me."

Rell accepted the call and brought the phone up to his ear. He tilted his head to the side, trapping the iPhone between his ear and shoulder. This way he could peel off the cash to pay Phil for the weed and Hennessy and talk to Juice at the same time.

"What it look like, big homie?" Rell said. He glanced at Lil Phil, who was now holding an iPhone in each hand, scrolling through a thread of text messages on the one in his huge right-hand.

There was a piece of scotch tape sticking out from the side of the other iPhone.

Chapter 8

"Did you tell anybody about what happened between you, Tamera, and Alexus in L.A.?" Juice said, frowning.

"Let me hit you right back, big homie. Five minutes," Rell said, and ended the call abruptly.

Juice looked down at his smartphone with an expression of sullen disdain for a moment and then slowly began to investigate the crowd again.

He had surprised Bubbles. While the double date had been underway at GAM's, a group of movers had transported the majority of her paintings from her beautiful Lake Forest home to the art studio he'd leased and opened without her fever having even the tiniest clue of its existence. He had paid his eighteen-year-old daughter, Shawnna, and Bubbles' friends and relatives. Shawnna's boyfriend, Bankroll Reese, and invited a few dozen of his wealthy associates (Reese himself had a net worth of $60 million) to the surprise art exhibit, and many of them had brought along their wives and mistresses. Three was security in case some unruly guest wished to stir up trouble. There was wine and cognac being served on silver trays, and GAM's was catering the event.

Bubbles had cried and laughed at the same time when he'd led her in and lowered his hands from over her eyes, and once the congratulatory cheers and applause had died down, she'd thanked everyone for coming and kissed him hard on the mouth.

Now she was standing in a cluster of family and friends in front of the most popular painting of them all, the one of a sneering Trump reaching down into a box full of kittens. Everyone was smiling and having a good time as they studiously perused the paintings – everyone but Juice.

A few minutes ago, Juice had received a text message from Bulletface, the rap megastar who'd given him the deal of a lifetime just last week.

"You know anything about Alexus fuckin w/Rell n Tamera?" the text from Bulletface read.

"Nope lil homie wouldn't do no shit like dat Neway," Juice had replied, and then he'd immediately phoned Rell to find out who'd opened their mouth about what went down in that dark dressing room at the Deja and D-Boy concert in Los Angeles last week. And Rell had essentially hung up in Juice's face.

"You good, Unc?" It was Kev, Juice's nephew. He was standing next to Juice, a lowball glass of Hennessy in one hand, his smartphone clutched in the other.

"Yeah," Juice said. "Yeah, I'm good." He glanced at this iPhone again, then turned to Kev. "It's good to see you back in your element, nephew. You was almost out for the count, but I see you done bounced back like good crack."

Three months ago, Kev had taken four bullets in an attempt on his life, and for two or three teeth-clenching days, the family had hoped and prayed for him to pull through. Now he stood next to Juice in a dapper gray suit-and-tie, looking stronger than ever, albeit twenty or so pounds lighter.

"Tara picked out this suit," Kev said, holding the tie out to study its two-tone diagonal gray stripes. Tara was his wife, the woman who'd stuck by his side through every grueling moment of recovery. She was in the group with Bubbles and Barbie, clad in a one-shouldered dress that one might expect to see at a red-carpet event. "Shawnna told her all the guys had to three-piece it up."

"It's a special occasion," Juice said.

"Man, I didn't know Bubbles had talent like this," Kev commented.

"You should see the one of Michelle Obama she got in her living room. I look at that picture more than I look at the TV."

"What was up with that trip y'all took to Cali? I know something good happened, 'cause it's been flooded ever since y'all came back. Reese dumped fifty bricks on me this morning. Fifty of 'em. Blew me with that pack, on my kids."

"Somebody might've just fucked that whole play up," Juice said in a low, contemptuous tone. "I got the plug hitting me up asking about his wife getting fucked backstage at a concert."

"Who, Alexus?"

"Yeah. She got drunk and gave up the pussy."

"Nawww."

"On cup, she gave up that pussy."

"To who?" Kev was all ears now.

"Don't tell nobody I told you this."

"Come on now, Unc. You know me better than that."

Juice hesitated for a brief moment, reluctant to spill this particularly hot serving of tea. "It was Rell," he said finally, knowing with complete certainty that it would stay between him and Kev. "Rell and Tamera."

"Rell *and* Tamera?" Kev whispered.

"Rell *and* Tamera," Juice said, nodding. "I looked over there a few times. Rell was eating Tamera's pussy while Alexus was riding him. Then Tamera rode him while Alexus sat on his mouth. Then he hit 'em both from the back, going from one to the other. I was on the other couch with Bubbles and Tirzah. But I saw it all with my own eyes."

"So you hit Tirzah too?"

"Nah, she wanted me to, but I didn't do it. Couldn't do Jah like that."

"Man. Hell naw. That's too crazy." Kev was shaking his head in disbelief, his eyebrows sitting way up on his forehead. "If I was him, I would've made her pay up for that. At least ten or twenty M's."

"Damn, you would've blackmailed her?" Juice bellowed fresh laughter into his nephew's face.

"Hell yeah, I would've blackmailed her ass. All that money she got. Shit, she could've gave him a hun'ed million and not lost a wink of sleep. Man, that's the wildest shit ever."

"I just hope it don't fuck up the business relationship."

"I feel you on that." Kev sipped his drink.

"I'm still looking for Marshall," Juice said. His grin was still present, but he was serious now – as serious as a fatal heart attack. You could have doubled the way America felt when those two hijacked commercial airlines went plunging into the World Trade Center Twin Towers and still have come up short. Because Juice had already lost his only son to gun violence this year, and knowing that someone was gunning for one of his last two living children was an understandably serious matter.

"He ain't coming back to Chicago," Kev said.

"You never know."

"Lil Mark set Lenny's whole house on fire so Marshall ain't coming back to pack his brother's shit."

"They came back from Detroit and shot my building up when Lenny got killed. Now Marshall done lost another brother. If he came at us over one dead brother, it seems logical that he'll do the same for another dead brother."

"How did he even get away?"

"Shit, they had choppas. And you know Wayno only had one hand to work with, 'cause he got shot in his right wrist when Jah got hit up. It was a few pistols against two AK-47s. We got lucky. They say Marshall ran into the alley behind Chandra's house. I guess he had a getaway car waiting there. Ain't nobody seen him since. Chandra said they came to her house with some big guns, but she didn't really think nothing of it until the other brother – DeAngelo, the second one who got killed – started looking out her front window. By the time she figured it out it was too late."

"You believe that shit?"

Juice shrugged. "I don't see why she would lie to me about it."

"What? Are you serious? Did you forget about how Dawn and Shawnna beat her ass out the strip club the night Junior got killed?"

No, Juice had not forgotten the severe beat down his daughters and their friends had given Chandra that fateful night at Redbone's. He just hadn't factored it into the Christmas Day shooting. Now he considered it, moving his crystal lowball glass in small circles and watching the ice cubes tornado around in his cognac. He lifted his head and cast his eyes around the room again, still thinking.

The walls and pillars were freshly painted In a glaring, light-reflecting oyster white. The smell of fresh paint hung in the air. It was a smell Juice ordinarily liked, but not now. At this moment, it was a smell that filled his nose, overpowering both the smell of alcohol on his breath and his nephew's strong cologne. Memories flickered through his mind like cards being shuffled by a habitual gambler, memories from the day Lee Wilkins Jr. was murdered. There was the shocking moment when his daughter, Shawnna, burst into a bathroom at Bankroll Reese's mansion and caught him squirting millions of potential brothers and sisters onto Chandra's naked bottom. Shawnna had also been naked-bottomed, making the encounter all the more embarrassing. The fact that Juice had been married to Shawnna's mother at the time was what led to Chandra's beat down, which had transpired in the VIP section at Redbone's Gentleman's Club mere minutes before Junior and his girlfriend were shot dead. To top it all off, when Juice had gone to break the news of their son's murder to his then wife, he'd found her in a very compromising position with the lesbian woman she ended up divorcing him to be with. That single day had been the absolute worst day of his life.

He had a feeling that terrible day might soon be eclipsed by an even worse day. Juice, who had never had a premonition in his life, was suddenly filled with a clear certainty that was both eerie and unnerving. *Within the next month or so, Marshall will be back in Chicago with his mind set on getting revenge for his two murdered brothers, and as soon as he sees Shawnna or Dawn, he's going to pull out his gun and start shooting with the intent to add an even worse day to Juice's timeline.*

Juice was drawn out of his reverie by the sight of Shawnna's contagious smile. She was walking toward him. Bankroll Reese was her shadow, his eyes fixed on his smartphone.

"Daddy," Shawnna said, and the word came out "*Deady*," because of the way she talked "Tell me why Bubbles is over there thinking she'd Van Gogh or somebody. She just sold one painting for a hundred thousand damn dollars, and they're offering three and four times that for the one with Trump's old racist ass."

"Stop being so loud," Juice said, throwing an arm around Shawnna's shoulders and pulling her in close.

"I just told her that," Reese said. He donned a black suit with a red tie that matched Shawnna's sweeping red sequined gown.

Shawnna flicked her eyes back at Reese. "You don't get to tell me what to do. When I push this baby out in five months, you can tell her what to do, but I'm only taking *suggestions* from you. And I'm also giving *you* suggestions. Suggestion number one: keep your eyes off all these bitches in here. Since you wanna tell me what to do."

The three men laughed mightily at Shawnna's next-level craziness.

Kev said, "Better keep your eyes off all these bitches in here."

"Nigga," Reese said, "I wouldn't look at another woman's shoes with this psycho around. I wouldn't even look at a woman on TV with Shawnna in the same building."

"Happy wife, happy life," Shawnna chirped with a prideful smirk. "Oh, wait— you ain't put a ring on it yet. Happy girl, happy world." She nodded, proud of her newly-coined phrase.

"As soon as you push my daughter out," Reese said, "I'm getting you put on some medication. Some *serious* medication."

"You ain't getting me put on nothing."

"We'll see about that." Reese looked up from his phone, beaming. "I'm slipping pills into all those pickles you be eating. Juice, you should see how many pickles she eats every single day.

"I know." Juice chuckled. "That's the same thing her mama ate when she was pregnant with her and Dawn."

"Speaking of Dawn," Shawnna said, "her and Wayno are catching a flight back here to Midway at 5:30. They'll be home by nine."

"They're coming home already?" Juice said, confused. He'd given Wayno $10,000 to leave Chicago for a while. Three days was not a while.

"Dawn is acting sick," Shawnna said as she raised her iPhone. "She lied and told Wayno she's coming down with the stomach flu, but this is the real reason she's getting on that plane." She went to her Snapchat app and pressed play on someone's video clips.

It was his girlfriend's younger cousin, Tamia.

In the first short video, Tamia stood next to Cage, aiming her phone at his dresser mirror while he lotioned his torso and arms.

Juice said, "She's leaving Jamaica because her ex-boyfriend is putting on lotion in the mirror?"

"Keep watching," Shawnna said in a tone of voice that indicated something better was on the way.

Juice did keep watching. Kev leaned in and watched, too.

They didn't have long to wait. The very next video showed Tamia sucking Cage's dick, taking it deep in her mouth and then pulling all the way back. There were three more videos of her fellating him (the best blowjob Juice had seen in a long time), and after that, there were videos of Cage fucking her in various positions. She was like Pinky the Pornstar in bed. A real screamer.

Tamia's motive for having sex with Cage immediately registered in Juice's mind. "She's mad about Dawn going to Jamaica with Wayno," he said, more to himself than anything.

"Mm-hmm." Shawnna nodded. "That's what I'm thinking. But you really can't say for sure. Tamia is a certified thot. A super thot. She's put up a few videos like this on her Snap. One time she put up a video of some W.I.C. City boys running a train on her in a Parkway Gardens apartment. That one was on Instagram. They suspended her account for a month for that stunt."

"She got a *fat* ass, though," Kev said, pulling out his own phone. "What's her name on Snapchat?"

"I can't remember." Shawnna scanned the crowd. "Let's find Tara and ask her."

The four of them laughed, and Shawnna walked off into the crowd in her shiny red gown. Juice watched her for a time, then swept his eyes around the room, searching through the faces mindlessly. He saw the people without really seeing them. He was lost in that formidable premonition, and wondering if Chandra, his old side chick, had played a role in the Christmas Day shooting that had targeted Dawn and Shawnna. Then Bubbles appeared at his side and kissed him on the cheek.

"Tirzah's on her way to Michigan City to be with Tamera and Rell," Bubbles said. "She just Facetimed me saying she wasn't staying at the hospital with Jah while his ex-girl is up there."

"You having fun?" Juice was looking down behind Bubbles and fighting the urge to grab her thick derriere and give it a firm squeeze.

"Of course I am," Bubbles said softly. She moved before him and cupped his face in her hands, and for a moment she gazed into his eyes and smiled. Then she kissed him, looking at him with a peculiar thoughtful scrutiny. "You amaze me sometimes. A lot of times, actually."

"I do my best."

"Your best is more than most men would do. You make me feel the way I'm supposed to feel. I can't thank you enough for that."

"I think you can," Juice said. He rested a hand on her lower back and grinned. He couldn't seem to stop grinning. "You can start by taking some lessons from your cousin."

"Yuck." She laughed. "You saw it already?"

He nodded. "Shawnna just showed us."

"I'm kicking Tamia's ass. That girl has zero fucks to give."

"It looked like she knew what she was doing."

"I mean, she *should* know what she's doing. All the dick she's sucked, she should be the next Superhead by now. I don't think she should be broadcasting it to the whole damn city."

"She got Superhead beat."

"I just sold another painting to Barbie's boyfriend. Three hundred and forty-five thousand dollars!" her eyes gleamed with excitement. She was still holding his face in her soft hands. Her Chanel perfume filled his nose. "You know, without you springing this whole art show thing on me, I would never have tried to sell any of my work. They're putting 'Trumpster' in his restaurant in Decatur, Georgia. I guess the other one will be in their house."

"I'm proud of you, baby."

"Is this spot mine now?" Bubbles asked, moving her hands to his wide shoulders. "Or did you just rent it out for the day?"

"It's yours. I signed a one-year lease."

"For how much?"

"Does it matter?" Juice said. Then, a second later, "It's $9,250-a-month, but to me, it's worth it. I paid the first and last month's rent. I'll pay the rest——"

Bubbles grabbed his face and kissed him again, right in front of their guests, and when their lips separated this time he saw tears in her eyes.

"I fucking love you," she said, and sniffled. Her daughter walked over, noticed she was on the verge of crying, and patted her on the back.

"I love you back," Juice said, really meaning it. The past six months had been a whirlwind of intense ups and extreme downs, and through it all Bubbles had remained his biggest source of happiness, like a circle of light at the end of a long tunnel. She had gone from being his favorite stripper to being his loyal girlfriend. He loved her for being her.

"Big Nasty," Ra'Mya said, planting her fists on her hips and scowling up at him, "why you got my mama over here crying? She's supposed to be smiling right now. You're ruining her makeup."

Still grinning, Juice handed his lowball glass to Kev, stuffed his hand in the left-hand pocket of his pants, and lowered his left knee to the tile floor.

Ra'Mya's eyes lit up, and she screamed for Shawnna, who appeared just as Juice was flipping open the small black square ring box.

The room became an oyster-white gallery of applause, cheers, and smartphone camera flashes. Juice took his lady's left wrist in his hand and looked up at her honey-brown face, which suddenly seemed to be locked in on expression of bliss mixed with an indescribable sort of shock.

"Oh my God," Bubbles said.

"I'm sure you know how much I love you and that little brat of yours," Juice began, "but I want to make sure that you both are around to raise my blood pressure until my blood stops pumping altogether." He was smiling, and now the smile broadened. "I have a question to ask you, Lakita Thomas, a question that is pure in my heart right now, a question that absolutely must be asked. Lakita Thomas, will you marry me?"

Bubbles nodded and said yes five or seven times, and Juice slipped a seven-carat cushion-cut diamond ring onto her finger. He heard Shawnna give Reese a cheerful yes, but he hardly noticed it as he stood and threw both arms around Bubbles in a bear-hug. He gave her one long passion-driven kiss and then a barrage of equally passionate pecks, lifting her off her feet. He had set out to make this the most special afternoon of her life, and judging from the beaming smiles on her and her daughter's face, his plan was a massive success.

Chapter 9

Tamia had just finished drying off after a nice long bubble bath. She had muted her cell phone shortly after she and Cage walked into her Spaulding Avenue apartment because just about every person she knew was calling and texting her about the Snapchat sex scene. Now, as she stood at her bathroom sink, wrapped in a fluffy bath-robe she'd stolen from a hotel a few months back, applying a clear gloss over her cherry-red lipstick to give it that special shine, she gazed at her reflection and asked herself a question.

"Why did I put that on Snapchat?" she said aloud, and in the next breath she answered, "Because that dirty hoe stole what was mine, that's why."

She smirked triumphantly and went on perfecting her lips, ig-noring her phone as it continuously lit up on the red faux fur lid of her toilet. Her mind went to the money she would be making tonight at the strip club. Although she'd told Cage the truth about how she was making money these days, she had not been honest about the amounts. She had actually made close to $3,500 at the strip club, and Juice had paid her $5,000 for the pick-ups and drop offs. She still had every dollar of the cash she'd gotten from Juice. Hopefully some more bands would come her way tonight. She was, in her bi-ased opinion, the baddest bitch to hit the stage at Redbone's Gen-tleman's Club since the legendary Bubbles, and she planned on go-ing way harder than her stingy, penny-pinching cousin.

Tamia was cleaning her ears with a Q-Tip when she heard a knock at the door. "Get that for me, Cage," she shouted. When the knock came again, she trashed the cotton swab, scooped up her purse and phone, and went out to answer the door.

She found Cage on the sofa, out cold with a sliver of drool hang-ing out the side of his mouth. He had the hood of his hoodie tied tight around his head, one hand was buried in his sweat-pants, and one of his sneakers was upside-down next to the coffee-table.

"Knew you couldn't hang," Tamia muttered as she approached the door, tying her bathrobe shut not only to hide her red-lace thong and bra, but also to protect her body from the cold air on the other side of the door. "Who is it?" she barked.

"It's me," a man said, but Tamia didn't immediately place the voice.

"I'm me; who the fuck are *you*?

"It's Lil Mark."

Tamia's eyes widened. A fist of fear closed around her heart. Her breath paused in her throat, like a burglar stopped in his tracks by the sound of a floorboard creaking under his feet.

Last Friday, she had been in the passenger's seat of Wayno's Chevy Suburban when Lil Mark, who was in the back seat with a long black assault rifle on his lap, had lowered his window and murdered a man named Styro. The bright flashes and loud explosions of gunfire from the big gun had come very close to making Tamia pee her pants. She remembered with hellish clarity the way the bullets had shaken the big man and blew great mists of blood out of his back.

Reluctantly, she unlocked the door and opened it a couple of inches to peer outside. She found Lil Mark and another young black man standing on the stoop, dreadlocks as long as the strings of a mop head dangling down around their heads. Lil Mark was the same age as Cage, and the guy next to him looked even younger. The thing that struck Tamia as out of the ordinary was that the two boys were so *fresh*. From their fitted baseball caps to their leather Pelle Pelle coats to their jeans and Jordan sneakers, everything they had on looked brand-new.

Tamia smelled money.

She glanced back at Cage, saw that he hadn't moved an inch, and turned back to Lil Mark.

"What do you want?" she said. "I got company."

"Damn, I can't come in?" Lil Mark said.

Tamia sighed and threw another glance at Cage. "Be quiet, okay? Go straight to my bedroom, sit on the bed, and don't touch any of my shit." She let them in and quickly shut the door. Her eyes stayed on Cage until they were both in her bedroom, then she went in behind them.

Lil Mark never followed orders. He was standing at Tamia's wooden dresser with his back to her when Tamia walked into the bedroom and locked the door behind her. His friend sat on the foot of her bed, scrolling through Instagram on his smartphone. In the reflection of her dresser mirror, Tamia saw that Lil Mark had dumped a bag of pills on the dresser-top. He looked up, and a slow smile spread across his face. His stared into the eyes of Tamia's reflection and offered her a nod that was little more than a very slight tilt of the head.

"What do you want?" Tamia repeated. "And when did you start dressing all Doug E. fuckin' Fresh?" She turned to the boy on her bed with giving Lil Mark the time to reply. "Hey. Who are you?"

"That's Lil Luke," Lil Mark said. He turned around. "You know his daddy, don't you? The music producer?"

She searched her memory, trying to rummage through the smog of weed and tequila to retrieve the name of a music producer, but she couldn't do it. In fact, she couldn't think of anything other than the man Lil Mark had gunned down in the midst of a snowstorm five nights ago.

"You know Luke. Luke from off Trumbull."

Tamia looked at Lil Luke again, and this time her eyes widened. He was looking up at her now, pocketing his phone.

"Your dad is Luke? The one who used to fuck with Dawn?"

Lil Luke nodded. There was no denying the resemblance. He might have been a shade or two darker, but he looked just like his father.

"You showed out on Snapchat," Lil Mark said, and chuckled. "Showed *out*."

"Whatever," Tamia said, but with no real force. She said it simply because it was something to say. Her mind was coming up with yet another vengeful plot to spite Dawn Wilkins.

"You fuck with the X, don't you?" Lil Mark asked. "I brought over some triple stacks. Just bought these bitches too. I ain't even popped one yet."

"Is that why you came over here? To see if I wanted to buy a pill?"

"We got tired of waiting for the nigga Marshall to show his face in the hood," Lil Mark said, placing a small blue pill on his tongue. He swallowed it. "We heard he was back in the city, but we ain't seen him nowhere. We drove all up and down 16th all up and down Douglas, all up and down Roosevelt, Homan, Trumbull, Christiana, Spaulding, Millard, Central Park. Ain't a soul seen that man."

"Then we watched that Snap action," Lil Luke said.

"On Cup, though," Lil Mark said, grinning. "I see why Cage out there comatose. You sucked his soul out."

Neither one of you lil boys are ready for this, Tamia thought. She opened her bathrobe and let it fall to the carpet. She put on a coy little smirk as she went to her nightstand to set her purse down, and before she could even turn around, Lil Mark was behind her, pressing the front of his jeans against her ass and kissing the nape of her neck. She had on a pair of five-inch heels— not the knock offs she usually wore, but real seven-hundred-dollar Prada stilettos-- and they put her at the perfect height for Lil Mark to grab her waist and slide right in, which he clearly wanted to do at the moment.

"Damn, you smell good," he said, reaching around to grope her B-cup breast.

She pushed his hands away and crawled up onto her queen bed, looking back at him and Lil Luke. She had a number of tricks she could do with her ass, and one of her favorites was making one cheek go up while the other went down. Rapidly. She did it and smiled at the boys' elated reactions.

"Aw, hell yeah," Lil Luke said with a mixture of surprise and guttural hunger. He tore off his coat and stood up, pulling a hefty rubber-banded pile of cash. "I got a hot fifty for you."

"Fifty ain't gon' do a damn thing for me," Tamia said, still bouncing her bountiful derriere. "Give me two of them double-stacks, and I need more than fifty. I ain't no fifty-dollar hoe."

Lil Luke transferred the rubber band to his wrist and peeled off two crisp hundred-dollar bills. He handed the bills to Tamia, and she put the cash in her knockoff Michael Kors bag.

"That's for both of us," Lil Luke said, returning the stack of cash to the right-hand pocket of his True Religion jeans. He was staring wantonly at her as she kneeled on the bed, sitting on the backs of her legs.

Lil Mark brought her two pills that had the face of Louisiana rapper Kevin Gates printed on them. "I ain't got no double-stacks," he said, taking off his coat and tossing it on top of Lil Luke's. "These triple. They call these I Don't GetId. Have you geeked up all night?"

Tamia nodded and looked from the two pills on her palm to Lil Luke. "How old are you?" she asked, regarding him with an accusatory squint.

"I'm sixteen, why? I've been countin' money and fuckin' gown bitches since I was thirteen. You know who my daddy is."

"You ain't got to get all defensive." Tamia shot a quick glance at the doorknob to make sure she'd locked it, then turned back to the two boys, smiling coyly. "Okay, listen. I'm your——" she pointed at Lil Mark "——cousin if Cage wakes up before y'all leave. I just started fuckin' with him today and I don't want him looking at me like a thot on our first day together."

The boys agreed to the stipulation and produced condoms from their jeans pockets. Tamia put one of the pills on her night stand, gave the other one back to Lil Mark, and moved to her hands and knees.

"Why you give it back?" Lil Mark asked.

"The girls at the club said it works better if you put it in...you know."

"You want me to put it in your ass?"

She nodded, too embarrassed to actually voice the request. Lil Mark didn't seem to mind. He slid her thong down around her thighs and thumbed the pill right into her butthole, while Lil Luke scooted across the bed and positioned himself so that her head was right over the bulging crotch of his jeans. She lifted Lil Luke's shirt and kissed on his well-sculpted abdomen while he undid his Louis Vuitton belt, pushed down his jeans and boxers, and freed his erect member. It sprang out and hit his abdomen with a light *thwack*, and Tamia chuckled at the sound it made as she picked it up in one closed fist and sucked the head into her mouth.

Sixteen or not, Lil Luke was one of the most well-endowed youngsters Tamia had ever fellated. She sucked as tightly and deeply as she could, using a lot of spit. Lil Mark smacked her on the ass, slid his hard member into her pussy, and slowly began to fuck her. She had half-expected Lil Mark to go hard and fast like all of the other young men she'd fucked in the past, but he really took his time, as if he was only warming up while she sucked off his friend.

Hardly three minutes had passed when Lil Luke's dick succumbed to'Tamia's tight mouth. She gave another little chuckle as she sucked on the head and stroked his twitching erection in both hands. She sucked until she could no longer feel the jets of warm semen shooting up into her throat, then took her mouth off him, swallowed, and squeezed one last drop out of him that she immediately licked up. She played with that last globule of semen, swishing it between her front teeth. She knew it was the taste of the sixteen-year-old's cum that made her orgasm and cream all over Lil Mark's dick a moment later. She looked between her legs and saw her orgasmic juices hanging there like the strand of saliva she'd seen lynched from the corner of Cage's mouth a few moments ago.

"You the baddest bitch I done fucked with, li'l mama," Lil Luke proclaimed as he got out of bed, smiling contentedly. "Got the best head too. I ain't never nutted that fast."

"That's what I want," Lil Mark said as he stepped back and gave her ass another sharp smack. "Nigga, look at how wet her pussy is. Come look at this shit. It's hanging like some pizza cheese, bruh. On cup." He got on the bed and moved to where Lil Mark had lain.

There was an intense tingling sensation in Tamia's rectum, sending slow, throbbing waves of pleasure throughout her body. She had Lil Mark grab the TV remote, turn to a music video channel, and raise the volume. She felt the overwhelming need to moan, and she didn't want Cage to wake up and hear her moaning.

She took the condom off Lil Mark's dick and jerked it in her hands. She decided it was about the same length as Lil Luke's, though not nearly as girthy. She took it into her mouth and sucked it like her life depended on it, bobbling and twisting her head so fast it must have seemed like a blur to Lil Mark.

He lasted a minute or two longer than his friend, then put his hand on the back of Tamia's head and thrust his hip up off the bed. The head of his dick was lodged in her throat when he ejaculated. At the same time, Lil Luke, having regained his erection, pushed and prodded his way into her asshole.

Tamia gave herself over to a second o–gasm - a particularly stron– one - and gagged on the semen she was trying to swallow. The cum shot out of her nose. She unplugged his still-gushing phallus from her throat and used her wrist to wipe the cum-snot from her nose. Neither of the boys seemed to notice the sex blooper, and seconds later, she was lapping up the cum she'd missed.

When he got hard again, she sucked another load out of him. This time she swallowed without any mishaps, and Lil Luke took off his condom and sprayed his seed across her undulating derriere. She scooped the cum off her butt and licked it all off her fingers.

"Y'all gotta go," she said, standing up and checking her cell phone for the time. It was 5:50 p.m. They had been in the bedroom with her for about twenty-five minutes.

Lil Mark looked at her with a mixture of intrigue and disgust in his eyes as he put on his coat. "You're a *nasty* bitch," he said with a grimacing grin.

"So what?" Tamia had taken a container of wet wipes out of her purse and was using a tissue to wipe the traces of semen from her face, wrist, and ass. "I ain't ashamed of shit I do. I'm still a bad bitch at the end of the day. What's up with the nigga y'all was looking for? You say his name was Marshall?"

"Fuck that nigga," Lil Mark said.

Tamia shrugged indifferently. She trashed the tissue, put on her bathrobe, placed a silencing forefinger on her lips, and led the two dread-headed teenagers out to the living room door. To her surprise, Cage was in the exact same position he'd been in twenty-some minutes earlier, only the slobber that had hung from the corner of his mouth was now in a small puddle on her faux leather sofa.

She rushed them out the door, shut and locked it, and then leaned back against it, breathing out a sigh of relief. She stood there for a long moment with her headed tilted back on the door and her eyes shut. She could almost feel the drug racing through her veins now. It gave her something like a cocaine high, a high she hadn't experienced in months.

When she opened her eyes, she looked down at her smartphone. The screen was lighting up with yet another call, this one from her friend Chandra. She considered letting it ring to voicemail. Then she remembered that Chandra hated Dawn Wilkins just as much as she did.

Tamia answered the call as she started off toward the kitchen to get a cold glass of Kool-Aid. Her mouth was terribly dry all of a sudden, and she could feel a bit of semen in her throat.

"Bitch, what the fuck you want?" Tamia said

"Girrrrl!" Chandra said, and Tamia knew what was coming next. "Why in the hell did you post that on Snapchat?"

"'Cause I wanted to."

"You better delete that shit before they suspend that account. You do know they can do that, right? And you know word done probably got back to Dawn about you and Cage fuckin' in those videos."

"Good." Instead of the Kool-Aid, Tamia filled a glass with water from the faucet. "She should be just as surprised about me and Cage as I was about her and Wayno." She took a big gulp of water.

"I knew I liked you for a reason." Chandra blasted a laugh through the phone. "I hope that bitch is crying her eyes out right now. Fuck her and her sister. Oh, and speaking of her sister, Shawnna just got engaged to Bankroll Reese."

"Get the fuck outta here!"

"Yeah, girl, it's all on Facebook and Instagram. I saw it on Kev's page about thirty minutes ago. Shit, your cousin got engaged too. Juice and Reese proposed at the same time. You know I'm too jealous. Juice used to be my boo. Shawnna and Bubbles just got engaged to the two biggest bosses in the whole city."

For a moment, Tamia stood in stunned silence, letting the information line itself up in her drug-clouded brain. Had she just heard Chandra right? Had her big cousin really gotten engaged to Juice? And if Dawn got all bent out of shape over Tamia and Cage, might she be able to get Shawnna to make Reese fire Tamia from her new job at the strip club? Shit, would Juice stop letting her make those deliveries too?

"I think you might be right about me needing to take down those videos," Tamia said, finally looking down at her glass and twirling it between her fingers. "Gotta stay focused on the money. Fuck all the bullshit."

"I bet they hate your whole existence. First you took Kobe from Shawnna, and now you done snatched up Cage. Are you and him together-together? Like, for real?"

"He's knocked out on my couch right now."

"Let me see."

"How?"

"I'm pulling up right now."

"Bitch, are you for real?"

"Yep, I got my nigga with me too. Hope you don't mind."

Tamia was back in the living room, pushing aside the black vertical blinds and peering out the large picture window. Sure enough, Chandra was right there across the street, parking her tiny little Kia Soul.

"That midget-ass car," Tamia joked as she watched Chandra and a light-hued man get out of the car and com trudging toward her walk-up unit.

"Bitch," Chandra said, "don't start getting on my car the day you got your new truck. Yesterday you didn't even have a car. And don't let me get on that raggedy-ass Pontiac you had this summer, because I can go all——"

"Okay, okay, okay," Tamia said quietly. "You got me. Look, y'all can't come in here all loud. I told you this boy is in here asleep. And who is that nigga you got with you?"

"You don't know him."

"Who is he?" Tamia persisted.

"Marshall," Chandra said with an irritated suck of the teeth. "His name is Marshall. Now open up the damn door before we freeze to death."

King Rio

Chapter 10

The drinks were flowing in Krystal Cartwright's two-bedroom apartment. Tirzah had arrived about an hour ago in Jah's Benz, so now there were two white S550s parked out front, which was probably the main reason why there had been a dozen knocks at the door since Tirzah's arrival.

Tamera loosened up as soon as her sister walked in, and within minutes, it became clear that Rell would be the designated driver. He didn't mind the assignment. If anything, it worked in his favor. He was high off Kush and fully aware of everything going on around him.

Krystal had called in sick to Buffalo Wild Wings, where she worked as a shift supervisor, which meant there were two sets of sister– now - three redbones and a backbone. The four of them were at the card table in the dining room, each on their second or third cups of Hennessy or Remy. All three of the redbones had popped a Molly pill, but Tamera stuck to weed and cognac.

The fat man had pocketeI the iPhone with the small piece of clear Scotch tape sticking out from the side of it right after he'd pulled it out. After Rell paid him for the weed and Hennessy, Lil Phil had spent almost an hour on a phone conversation with a woman he called Poochie. During the call, Rell overheard enough to know that Poochie was the mother of at least two little girls, had a truck that Lil Phil was tired of putting in the shop for repairs, and was squandering the day away in a hospital room due to complications from lupus. Rell got the impression that Poochie was someone the fat man truly loved, and that maybe one or both of her daughters were biologically his. Then Phil talked for another twenty minutes with someone named Rico, who wanted to go and meet up with T-Walk at Manna's tonight. Phil didn't seem as much into this conversation. He kept trying to put an end to the call, but the guy on the other end didn't seem to want to let him go. Through it all, Rell just sat there on the loveseat and listened c–osely - as closely as he could with the music blaring from Krystal's computer, anyway. He smoked two blunts with the fat man and three Newports by himself.

He surfed the Internet on Tamera's phone and saw on Facebook that Juice and Bankroll Reese had proposed to their girlfriends, and that half the people he knew from the west side of Chicago were calling Tamia the new Superhead because of some video she'd shared on Snapchat.

The one thing Rell kept going back to was the GPS tracker. His phone's beacon was right underneath Tamera's as it had been ever since he'd hung up on Juice. His eyes had not deceived him. His iPhone 7 was in the fat man's left-hand pocket.

When the fat man was finally able to hang up on Rico, he sighed and looked and Rell, shaking his head. "Don't you just hate a bum-ass nigga?" he said in a disgruntled tone of voice. "This nigga wanna sit around like he wanna shop wit' me when all he really wanna do is beg for some free shit so he can sell it and buy some more Tunechi. Ain't that about a bitch?" He picked up the bottle of Remy Martin he'd cracked open at the start of his talk with Poochie and drained a quarter of it at a drought.

"The fuck is Tunechi?" Rell asked.

"That fake synthetic weed bullshit."

"Oh. K2."

"Yeah, that shit. They call it Tunechi out here." He looked at Rell as if he hadn't seen him until now. "You ain't from around here, is you?"

Rell shook his head.

"I can tell." Lil Phil nodded, and his jowls wobbled. He seemed to not have a neck between his head and shoulders. "I can definitely tell. You got swag. Like me."

Bullshit, Rell thought.

"I ain't from out here either," Lil Phil said. "I'm from Nap. Indianapolis. I was actually born in Chicago, then my mom moved down to Nap with my aunt Judy. I'm from 30th and Delaware out there. That's my hood. I was one of the only GD's in a hood full of Lords, out there winnin', on Larry. I had the '71 Impala, all silver with the blue guts of silver-and-blue, 30-inch Forgiato Mistos. That bitch had the chrome Forgiato grille, a 22-inch touchscreen co–puter - on Larry, I was shittin' on niggas the hard way. My li'l nigga

Jimmy had the burnt orange '75 Delta 88 on thirties. Man, my whole hood was stuntin'. That was two summers ago, whenI gettin slabs for $26,000 from my nigga Spradley when everybody else was payin' $35,000 and up. One month I ran through ten whole thangs by myself."

"So what happened? How you end up out here?"

"Shit, I'm on the run. Feds raided my crack-house, my girl's house, my nigga Jimmy's house, my granny's house... My girl got hit with a brick of boy, five bricks of girl, and over $400,000. They took all three of my Chevys, my Benz truck, and my house. My nigga Twin got killed in a shootout with the Feds when they ran in on him. They indicted seventeen niggas from my hood. I'm the only one still on the run."

"What happened, somebody set y'all up?" Rell asked, leaning forward to roll another cigarillo of Kush on the coffee table. He was trying to keep Lil Phil talking.

"Hell yeah," Lil Phil said. "This gay-ass nigga from Anderson, a nigga named Jay Smoove. He wore a wire on Jimmy and bought a half a brick with some marked money the Feds had him use. I told Jimmy not to trust that nigga. I was in Westville prison with Smoove -same joint I met the n–gga Rico in - and Smoove was in there laid up with two or three different fags."

"That's crazy."

"I think somebody sent him at us, somebody in the streets. We had a lot of haters. Especially after we came through the Circle City Classic and shut that bitch down in our old schools. I think Spradley was even hatin' on us, and he was the bird-man. Shit he's *still* the bird-man. He got that real cartel plug. I tried to fuck with the nigga last week on some shit, but he was spinnin' me so I fucked with some Latin Kings from up this way. Bitch charged me $10,000 for a nine-piece. I'm still shitty about that."

"I feel you," Rell said, simply for the sake of saying something.

Lil Phil tossed another fifty-dollar bag of Kush to Rell. "I don't want you to think I'm tryna smoke up the sack I just sold you. Just keep that one for you," he said.

King Rio

Rell nodded. "So," he asked, digging for more info, "the girl you talked to –n the phone - is that the same one who got caught with all that dope and money?"

"Nah. I got two kids by Poochie. Me and her broke up a while back, in 2011, I think. She is the reason I didn't get caught up in that raid, though. I was at the hospital with her when the Feds hit. She had just had a lupus attack the night before, same shit she went in for yesterday. That's why I came out here to be with her."

"You don't think the Feds will be watching her to see if you come to visit your kids?"

"I was in the joint when both of my daughters was born, so my name wasn't on the birth certificates," Lil Phil explained, and he gulped down some more Remy. "And she never put me on child support. Shit, I was sending her ten or fifteen racks every other month. Even when I was in the joint, I was taking care of my kids." He paused, then smiled. "Except for a few months I had to make that bitch starve." Lil Phil's smile took on a little twist as he spoke the last sentence. The twist had a look both spiteful and derisive.

Rell chuckled and shook his head slowly. "What made you do that?"

"She started fuckin' with this broke nigga my hood was into it with. A nigga from Crew Life named Ladon. She knew he had robbed us before I went to the joint, but she was still fuckin' with the nigga."

"That's fucked up," Rell said laconically.

"It's deeper than that, though. I found out in the joint that Ladon was the same nigga who shot up my C^{he}velle on 38th Street and killed my nigga Dame. Shot me in my left leg too."

"You ever catch up with that nigga when you got out?"

That spiteful, derisive smile resurfaced on the fat man's face. "Did we catch him? We caught him and did him *bad*, on the *hood*." Every time he said the word *him*, it came out sounding like *eem*. "Did eem bad". "We ran into that nigga at the rink and stomped his ears together. He was in the hospital for the rest of the year. Had to learn how to walk again and everything. Then I took his bitch and had a–baby by her - that's my third daughter. He got some payback, though. Whacked my nigga at the liquor store. He got seventy-five years for that shit."

Rell winced at the notion of a seventy-five-year prison sentence. He'd done some time himself, and he'd been around men with that kind of time to serve. All of them had seemed to believe that they would be going home within the next few years. They all had some kind of appeal in the works, or some sort of motion being typed up to present to the courts. Yet if you took the time to stare into their eyes when you asked them about their release dates, you could very easily see miles upon miles of deep emptiness in their glazed-over pupils. Essentially, they were dead men, wandering through their daily prison lives trying to convince others that they were just as much alive as the men who were *really* going home in the next few months or years.

"You in the game?" Lil Phil asked. "I saw that Benz out there with the Illinois plates, and since I'm used to seeing all the other cars out there in the parking lot, I'm willin' to bet the Benz is yours."

"It's mine," Rell said, and that was all.

"You in the dope game?"

"I dibble and dab here and there. I bought the Benz with the money my ole man left me when he passed."

"You buy that other Benz too?"

Rell nodded. It was a lying nod. "He left enough to set me straight for a while. A million and some change." Deciding this was the best moment to broach the subject he'd been skating around for the last ten minutes or so, he added, "I know you're still in the game. I saw that other phone you pulled out at first. You got *two* iPhones? What, you use one to trap on and one for family?"

"Nah, nah." Lil Phil pulled out the –ther iPhone - Rell's iPhone. "I was actually just trying to figure out the password to this damn phone."

"You lost the password?"

"It was never mine to have in the first place."

"Why you say that?" Rell pressed. He was on the edge of his seat, staring not at his iPhone but at the man who was holding it in one open palm.

Lil Phil was concentrating on the phone, trying another password. "I, uhh..." He paused, and for two impossibly long seconds, Rell waited with his eyes wide open and fixed on the fat man's mouth, anxious to hear what would come out of those fat fish-lips. "It was actually stuck up under there with some gum and tape. It was kinda hanging off, and I saw it, so I t'ok it. I don't think he even knew it was under there. I met up with him at the gas station to loan him some cash to get a new truck. He went after the nigga who killed my aunt Rissa's son in Chicago. He said he shot the nigga, but they shot his truck up as he was driving off."

"And you found the phone under his shot-up truck?"

Phil nodded vehemently. "It was just hanging there. I had him waitin' on me for like a half hour. When I pulled up, he was in the gas station restroom, and the phone was just hanging there with a big glob of gum stuck to it. I asked him about it when he came out, and he swore up and down I was tryna pull one over on him."

So the man who'd shot Jah was the fat man's father. Rell could hardly hold back his smile. He lit the blunt he'd just finished rolling, pulled out his massive wad of cash, and said, "How much you want for the phone?"

Phil lifted his head and gaped at the ash in Rell's hand. "Damn," he said. "I don't know why you would wanna buy a locked phone, but I'll definitely sell this bitch to you. Gimme uhhhh...a hundred. Nah, nah, I'll just take fifty. Gimme fifty and it's yours."

As Rell was wriggling loose the fifties, the Cartwright sisters, apparently having won a game, jumped up from the card table, shouted out that Flint was in this bitch, and began to dance with their hands on their knee, their backs arched inward, and their tongues sticking out between their teeth. Tirzah, not a sore losing bone in her body, got up and twerked with them, while Tamera laughed and collected the cards.

Phil leaned forward and spoke in a whisper. "I fucked *both* of them bad-ass bitches, on the hood. Keyanna *and* Krystal. The bitch

Keyanna charged me two hundred for the pussy and then stole another hundred out of my pocket when I was asleep. I didn't even trip, though. They the baddest li'l bitches out here, and me and my li'l brother are the only ones that done fucked 'em."

"You hit Krystal too?" Rell handed over the fifty, and Phil handed over the phone.

"On Larry, I did," Phil said. "I had been tryna get her to let me taste the pussy for the longest, but she wouldn't go for it. Th–n one night - this was a fe– months ago - I came over here with some Remy that I had dropped like four or five X-pills in. Her thirsty ass drank most of the bottle." That spiteful derisive smile was on his lips again. "Next thing you know, I was on the bed with the bitch, suckin' the juice out that pussy. I fucked her, then my brother came in and fucked her, and when I came through here the next day, she acted like she didn't even remember the shit."

"That's crazy," Rell said, meaning it was crazy that this sick fuck had drugged Krystal for sex. He decided right then that Lil Phil would die w–th Big Phil - or whatever the hell his father's name was.

Chapter 11

Lil Mark had never been in a Corvette before. Not until this morning, when his childhood friend Richard Luther Perry, alias Lil Luke, had pulled up to the convenience store on the corner of 16th and Drake in the metallic silver ZR1 that they were now breezing down Douglas Boulevard in.

The time of day was just 6:54 p.m., and the sky was already nearly black with night. Lil Mark had a heavy black .50-caliber Desert Eagle resting on his lap, and his vigilant brown eyes were peering at every face and into every car and truck they passed.

"What you plan on doin' for New Year's Eve?" Lil Luke asked.

"Adding to the body count," Lil Mark answered, and offered his friend a small, tentative grin.

"The fucked up part about it is you ain't even playin'. You really mean that shit."

"I mean everything I say."

"You know, it's been a while since I've been in the hood. Who y'all into it with now?"

"Shit, who we *not* into it with," Lil Mark said placidly. "You know how this street shit go. We got opps everywhere. The Breeds, the Souls, the Bricks, the cops. Fuck all of 'em."

The "Bricks" was a derogatory term for the Gangster Disciples. Lil Mark had shot and killed three of them this year and wounded ten others. Altogether (so far as he knew, anyway), he had killed fourteen men and wounded well over thirty others in 2016, and he wasn't opposed to taking another life in honor of his beloved block, 15th Street and Trumbull Avenue, before the year came to a close.

"I'm surprised Tamia went like that," Lil Luke said, sounding genuinely surprised as he stopped at the light on Douglas and Kedzie. He looked over at Lil Mark. "That bitch is too bad to be going like that. She cute as fuck, ass crazy-fat...I don't understand it. I would've tried to make her my bitch if I'd have met her without seeing that video."

"Hoes gon' be hoes, bruh. Can't turn a hoe into a housewife."

"So what's up with Juice? My pops told me Juice stepped down and gave up his slot to Big Zo."

Lil Mark nodded, leaned forward, and peered closely at two tall men on his side of the street. They turned out to be just two of the four corner hustlers from off Millard Avenue. He sat back. "Yeah, Juice got too much going on to be running the mob. Big Zo just got out the joint. He got the same status Juice got, so Juice blessed him with ten bricks and let him take over. Big Zo deserved that slot. You know his two sons, Lil Zo and Roddy, got killed. He was in Stateville when that shit happened, didn't even get to go to the funerals."

"Roddy was my li'l nigga," Lil Luke said morosely.

"Mine too."

"Did they ever find out who whacked him?"

"They say Jah did it."

"Think he really did it?"

"Ain't no tellin'. You know Jah get down like I get down."

"I see why Juice really fell back, though. That nigga got *Bubbles*. I wouldn't come outside for ten years if I had that thick bad mu'fucka in the house with me. "You know who Bubbles reminds me of?" He didn't leave room for a guess. "That big-booty girl in the movie *ATL*."

"Big Booty Judy?"

"Naaah. That was Buffie the Body. I'm talkin about the one T.I.'s li'l brother was tryna holla at when she walked out that restaurant and couldn't get her car started, that pretty-ass redbone." He coiled his fingers around the steering wheel as if it had suddenly morphed into that sexy movie character. "He wouldn't even have Bubbles if he wasn't the birdman. You know it like I know it. He saved her from the strip club. My pops said she quit stripping the day she got with the big homie."

"Tell your pops I said keep Juice's name out his mouth." The ice in Lil Mark's tone of voice was palpable. He had a lot of love for Lil Luke, but he would –ill someone - –ell, anyone - for bad-mouthing Juice or any other high-ranking member of the Traveling Vice Lords, childhood friends included.

"I didn't mean it like that," Lil Luke muttered weakly.

"Don't matter how you meant it. Niggas get whacked for shit like that."

"You right, bruh."

"I know I'm right. Pull up on the side of them and top." Lil Mark pointed at a dark-colored Nissan that was idling at the curb near the corner of 16th and Homan.

There were men in the front seats, women in the back. As Lil Luke pulled up alongside the Nissan, Lil Mark saw that its male passengers were Apple and Colby, two of the TVLs off Trumbull. He gave them a nod and told Lil Luke to keep it moving.

"You that thirsty to shoot somebody?" Lil Luke asked.

"You ain't been out here in a while, li'l bruh. This shit serious. If you see a car you don't recognize, you gotta investigate. You never know if the niggas in that car got murder on their minds or not. End up like Head and Lil Dave if you want to. I ain't going to."

Lil Luke shot a brisk glance at Mark, appeared to steel himself, and said, "Guess I been in the suburbs too long. Shit done got real." He reached in his coat, pulled out a chrome revolver, and laid it on his lap. "You really think Marshall gon' come back through her after he done lost two brothers? He gotta be stupid as fuck to do that."

"He came through sprayin' once and tried to whack Juice's daughters. If he's dumb enough to do that, he's dumb enough to come back and do it again." Lil Mark squeezed his eyes shut for a brief moment and then opened them. The triple-stack ecstasy pill he'd taken must have really been packed with a triple-dose of MDMA, enough to free every bit of serotonin in his brain. His head was spinning, and there was perspiration on his brow, around his neck, and in his armpits. "Shit. That pill. I should've waited to pop that."

"It's that good?" Lil Luke asked.

"Hell yeah. Got my whole head spinnin'."

"I popped two X-pills before, and both times I didn't feel a damn thing."

"Then you must've popped the wrong kinda pills."

"Maybe so." Lil Luke seemed to ruminate about it for a moment, slowing the Corvette to a halt as the two cars directly ahead of them made a right into the parking lot of Redbone's Gentleman's Cl–b. "Fuck it - let me get one. Might as well roll a li'l bit. Ain't shit else crackin' out here."

"Everybody over there at Tweet Body's house. That's where we need to be," Lil Mark said, digging in his coat pockets to get the pills. He came up empty-handed. Next he checked his pants pockets, and again he didn't find the pills. "Shit," Lil Mark said.

"What?" Lil Luke said.

"I left 'em on Tamia's dresser. Damn. Hurry up and drive back over there before she fuck around and steal my whole sack."

The Brick Man 5

Chapter 12

"Bitch, are these X-pills?" Chandra asked as she picked up one of the small round blue pills from Tamia's dresser top and held it up in front of her face.

"Mm-hmm," Tamia said, and that was all she said, because she was on top of Marshall in the sixty-nine position with his dick sliding in and out of her throat.

Tamia hadn't planned on sucking Marshall's dick when he and Chandra had walked into her apartment almost an hour ago. Especially not with him having two black eyes and an obviously broken nose. He was short and bald-headed and the greenish-purple bruising under his eyes made him look anything but attractive.

They had sat on Tamia's bed and he had watched TV while she talked trash about Dawn and smoked a joint with Chandra. It was his confession that he also hated the Wilkins twins that had made Tamia take a liking to him, and when Chandra had suggested Tamia should let him get "summa dat Snapchat head" she had told him to lie back on the bed.

And now there he lay, balls-deep in her constricting throat, humping up into her mouth while his girlfriend stood at the dresser studying an ecstasy pill between her thumb and forefinger.

"Can I take one?" Chandra asked.

Tamia lifted her mouth up Marshall's long wet shaft until the head came out of her mouth with a loud wet pop. She began to jerk it rapidly in one tight fist. "These are my cousin's pills," she said, looking up at Chandra.

"I'll pay for it."

"You don't wanna take that. I'm rolling so damn hard right now, I can barely even take it." Tamia took Marshall's dick back into her mouth and started humping up into her throat again.

"There are one, two, three, four…almost twenty pills up here. You mean to tell me I can't buy one? Hell, I wanna roll too. I like––––"

Thump. Thump-thump-thump.

It was a knock on the bedroom door.

Tamia's eyes went wide. She quietly dislodged the hard phallus from her throat and looked at the door.

"Tamia! Open up the door," Cage said.

"Wait a minute," Tamia said, thinking up an excuse. "Chandra's in here with her boyfriend." She looked at Chandra. "Girl, hurry the fuck up."

"Okay, bitch," Chandra said, playing along.

"Can I warm up that pizza you got in the 'frigerator?" Cage asked.

"Yeah, go ahead," Tamia said, stroking Marshall's dick in her tight fist. "There's a case of Mountain Dew under the sink."

Just as Cage's footfalls began to fade away beyond the door, a ribbon of semen shot out of Marshall and glued itself to Tamia's face. She quickly closed her mouth around the ejaculating head and gave him a slap on the leg for not warning her. He then slapped his hands onto her ass and dug his fingers into the soft flesh as she sucked him dry.

His cum had exactly the sort of milkshake consistency Tamia craved. She sucked and stroked, sucked and stroked, and when it was all said and done, she stood before her dresser mirror and held open her mouth to look at the thick mess of cum on her tongue. It felt surprisingly heavy and looked like molten candle wax. She shut her mouth and swished the semen around until she heard the ding of her microwave going off, and then she tossed an ecstasy pill into her mouth and used the mixture of cum and spit to wash it down, eyeing the strip of white that went up one side of her nose and onto her forehead.

"Bitch, you need to be a pornstar," Chandra said. She still had the pill in her hand, and now she threw it in her mouth and swallowed it.

"Should've put it in your butt," Tamia said, and she was suddenly shaken by w–ld laughter - a sudden bright image of Chandra fingering a pill up into her anal cavity had come to her. Still laughing, she went to her nightstand, found a peppermint candy in her drawer, and put it in her mouth. She put on a pair of curve-hugging gray jeans and a red T-shirt after wiping the cum off her face. Then she unlocked the door, and Cage trotted in a moment later with a plate stacked high with slices of pepperoni pizza in one hand and a tall glass of iced soda in the other.

There was a ladder-back chair next to Tamia's closet door. Cage went to it and sat down. "Patron knocked me out," he grumbled and took a big bite out of a slice of pizza. He was still chewing when he added, "Think it was that Kush too. Perfect combo. Put me clean out."

"Mm-hmm," Tamia said in tones of skepticism. "Young ass. Talkin' about how you was all grown and shit. One blunt and some Patron took you right out the game. I should've dumped a bucket of water on your face." She stared at him with a crooked smile on her face and her hands on her hips, standing at the dresser while Chandra and Marshall sat by each other on the bed.

"I had a dream," Cage said, "about my uncle Styro. He handed me a bag full of money. I knew it–was a dream - don't know how I knew– but I knew - but I tried to hold on to it anyway."

Tamia gaped at him. Her mouth had fallen open when he said his uncle's name, and she was able to fix her shocked expression a millisecond before he looked up from his plate. She remembered him mentioning his dead uncle earlier, but she hadn't known the man's name. Now that she knew the dead uncle was Styro, she regretted having let Lil Mark into her apartment while Cage was asleep. She'd witnessed Lil Mark murder Styro in cold blood last week. Styro had lost control of his van in the snowstorm and slid off the road into a vacant lot just off 16th Street and Spaulding Avenue. He had stumbled through the snow, away from his van and onto the sidewalk, waving frantically at Wayno's red Suburban and shouting for help, only to be gunned down by a fellow Vice Lord for allegedly snitching on Jahlil Owens.

"I knew Styro," Marshall said. "He got killed the day before my oldest brother got killed last week. We used to buy our weed from Styro until his spot got raided."

"Yeah?" Cage said.

Marshall nodded his head solemnly. "Him and my brother Lenny was real cool. He used to come through and smoke blunts with us all the time. Y'all know who whacked him?"

"Nope. Police say his van either got ran off the road or he lost control of it. Somebody shot him up right after that. They hit him with some kinda assault rifle."

"I don't know who killed my brother." Marshall was lighting a Newport cigarette, gazing into the flame that stood between his lighter and the tip of the cancer stick. "I know who had it done, though. It was that Shawnna bitch. I wanna kill that bitch so fuckin' bad for that shit. We tried to whack that bitch on Christmas. That's how my other brother got killed."

"Sorry to hear that. I can't imagine losing both of my brothers."

"It's all good. They just set my brother's house on fire last night, but it's all to the good. I got a trick for they asses." There was a clear and cold threat in Marshall's words.

"Don't tell nobody y'all seen us together," Chandra said, getting up to leave. "These niggas out here been looking for Marshall, and I don't want them knowing where he's at."

"We ain't gon' say shit," Tamia said, and led them out to the front door. She hugged Chandra, drew back, and smiled. "You need to come up to Redbone's and hit the stage with me. Get some of that fast money."

"I'll think about it." Chandra, pulled open the door and left out ahead of Marshall. "Come kick it with me for New Year's Eve too," she shouted as she and Marshall headed down the walkway.

Then Tamia's mouth fell open again.

There was a silver Corvette parked across the street, just two spaces behind Chandra's tiny orange Kia Soul, and the two boys getting out of the silver Corvette were Lil Mark and Lil Luke. They noticed Marshall at the same moment he noticed them, and all three of them whipped out pistols. Lil Mark's huge gun looked like it could take off an elephant's leg with one pull of the trigger, and when he pulled the trigger, it sounded like it might actually blow the elephant to the moon.

Chandra turned and came running back to the door just as the gunfight began, but Tamia swung the door shut and locked it on her. "Cage! Get down!" Tamia shrieked as she dove to the floor.

Outside, the gunfire boomed like thunder. Tamia heard Chandra pounding on the door. Then a large hole appeared in the middle of her door, and Chandra stopped pounding.

King Rio

Chapter 13

Throughout the 30,000 square feet of interior space inside Blake King' Calabasas home only the finest materials h–d been used - marble, onyx, jade and a number of exquisite woods.

The estate featured in-laid marble floors, magnificent 22 karat chandeliers, vaulted ceilings, luxurious baths, a state-of-the-art theater, a culinary center, a spa, a sauna, a music recording studio, a private gym, and a wine cellar. The ballroom had a spacious full-service bar, a surround sound system and multiple television screens.

Blake had spent almost an hour in the gym after the marriage counseling session with Dr. Farr. Afterward he'd take in a long hot shower, put on a pair of Versace boxer shorts, his favored black-and-gold Versace robe, and horsebit-leather Gucci loafers. He'd sat in the theater and watched *Hidden Figures* while drinking Lean from a Styrofoam cup and trying to keep his mind off the throbbing pain in his heart. He'd sent Juice a text message asking about Alexus and Rell, knowing that even if the rumor was true, Juice wouldn't tell him, so but unable to dissuade himself from sending the text all the same. And then he'd pushed that dull throb in his heart aside. And reminded himself that he was Bulletface, the ordinary dope boy who had grown up poor in northwest Indiana, selling crack out of a trap house in his neighborhood and recording mixtapes to document the life of a young real nigga in his prime. Bulletface, who had gazed with awestruck eyes at the TV every time he saw Young Jeezy or Lil Boosie or Jay Z because he knew that they had risen from poverty to stardom, which meant he could also do it if he worked hard enough. Bulletface, who was now worth almost two billion dollars, had four multiplatinum albums, and an equal number of Grammys to his name. He was the CEO of the hottest record label in the industry right now. What the fuck was he doing sitting in his theater feeling all broken-hearted, while his wife was out with her friends at some Oprah event in Hollywood?

He ditched the Lean for some real-deal cognac (as Hennessy's latest choice for a celebrity spokesperson, he felt it only right that he drink some every now and then), put on his standard uniform of white Balmain shirt and jeans over white studded Christian Louboutin sneakers, added several diamond necklaces to the mix, and then FaceTimed Young Meach, a friend of his since elementary school. He was sitting in a chaise longue outside by the Olympic-size swimming pool when he made the call. His older brother, T-Streets, and two of their record company's female employees were chilling in the pool. There were two butlers, three maids, and five armed bodyguards standing around the pool. If Blake looked back he could see miles and miles of plush green trees and earth tones of brown landscape and the roofs of other California homes that weren't situated high up on a hill like his.

"What's stackin', bad?" Meach said, and Blake didn't even have to look at the phone screen to know that Meach was smiling; he could hear the smile in Meach's voice. Meach, the President of Moneybags Management, was also a successful rap artist. "Man, the fans been missing you out here, bruh. You gotta get back to it the bad way."

"All the shit I'm going through with Alexus," Blake said, shaking his head somberly. "I think she fucked Rell last week."

"Who?"

"One of the niggas we kicked it with at the last Deja and D-Boy concert."

"Oh." Meach looked away from the phone, seeming to consider it. "How in the fuck could she have done that?" His eyes were on Blake again. "Wasn't he with us the whole night?"

"That's the same thing Alexus said."

"Shit, it's true, ain't it?"

"I think so. But then again, I do remember holding my cup up to toast with them in the hallway, right outside the dressing room door. Rell and Juice had just came back from the restroom."

"Was Alexus there then?"

"I ain't sure. If she was, she didn't tell me."

"Did you ask her bodyguard? What's his name?"

"Byron."

"Yeah," Meach said. "The Jamaican nigga. You know he's like her shadow. Did you ask him?"

"Nah, but I'm about to," Blake said thoughtfully.

"Who put that bug in your ear in the first place?"

"Barbie told me about it."

Meach chuckled twice. "I ain't never known Barbie to lie. You know she still strips at Magic City in the A, and I know every stripper in there. But you gotta take into account that you and Barbie used to fuck. She might've just said that to piss you off, bruh. I wouldn't even pay that no mind."

"Barbie ain't never lied to me. That's the only reason I believed the shit."

"Yeah, but you know how exes be," Meach pointed out.

"I know," Blake sighed. He sipped from his cup of Hennessy and simmered with irritation. He was all the M-words: mid-twenties, muscled-up, mentally unstable, and at this particular moment, murderous. "All the shit really started when T-Walk came into the picture."

"You know he at the crib tonight, right?"

"Yeah?" Blake said with drawn-together brows.

Meach nodded. "At the same club y'all shot each other at. It just reopened a few weeks ago. It's Manna's now."

Blake became thoughtful. He took another fiery sip of Hennessy. His face tightened as the liquid fire poured down his throat.

"What's in that cup?" Meach asked. He was scrubbing a soft-bristled hairbrush forward on the top of his head.

"Hennessy."

"Since when you started back drinking liquor? I thought it was purple drank to the end."

"I needed it. Where you at?"

"At my grandma's house. I'm about to get dressed and hit the club, though. We gotta hit up Miami on the thirty-first. Club Liv. Everybody gon' be there for Ne– Year's Eve - 2 Chainz, Wayne, Chris Brown, and Nicki, too."

"That's really why you wanna go anyway, nigga," Blake said with a grin. "You should've just said her name first."

"Naaah," Meach said guiltily. "You know I rack with Meek."

"So what? They ain't even together no more."

"Yeah right."

"I ain't bullshittin'. She told Alexus it's over. Her and Meek got into it on her birthday."

"Bruh, I'm about to hit her in the DM like, 'hey, big booty.' On Angelo." Meach laughed a long "haaaa" and went on brushing his wavy black hair. White VVS diamonds blinged in the rose gold Rolex on his wrist. He was dark and handsome and, now that Blake thought about it, kind of Meek-Mill-ish.

"What club you going to tonight?" Blake asked.

"Manna's. I need to see T-Walk up close with my own two eyes. I still can't believe he's alive. Plus, everybody gon' be there. You already know that. Especially the GD's. You know they look at him like he's Larry Hoover."

One of the butlers was balancing a gold tray full of pre-rolled marijuana cigars on the palm of his hand. Blake waved him over, took a blunt, and let the butler light it for him. "Meach," he said, shifting his attention back to the phone, "don't tell nobody, but I'm about to get my cars flown to the Chicago airport, and I'll be right behind 'em on the G6. I'm coming to Manna's too. Fuck it. That's my city."

"Don't have us out here on no bullshit."

"I'm too rich to be on that. I'll put some cash on his head if it comes to beef. Shit, we just gave that nigga $10 million to get back on his feet; I doubt if he'll bite the hand that's feeding him."

Meach nodded carefully. "Just … keep your cool. I know the Hennessy drinking Blake is way different than the Lean-drinking Blake. Henny Blake'll catch a body."

"I ain't on that."

"Don't let that shit Barbie told you get under your skin. Her and T-Walk are like brother and sister. She probably just wants you and Alexus to break up so he can get back with Alexus and get both of 'em in on the money."

"A'ight. I'll hit you when I get there. Dub Life or No Life, nigga."

"The bad way," Meach said, and terminated the video call.

Blake made the necessary calls to arrange his trip to Chicago, and then he dialed the number to his wife's bodyguard. He got the voicemail and was about to call again when his phone rang with a FaceTime call from his wife.

"Baby, you are not going to believe this," Alexus said urgently. Her sexy green eyes were shimmering with tears. "My bodyguards were just killed on the expressway! I sent them to pick up Enrique, and somebody in an eighteen-wheeler just about flattened them in my Rolls-Royce. It was that fucking Julio Chaves. I know it…"

Alexus went on blaming the incident on Julio's Mexican drug cartel, which was currently at war with her drug cartel, but Blake wasn't buying any of it. There was only one person who had a motive to silence the bodyguards, and that person was Alexus Costilla. She had silenced them to keep them from telling him what had happened between her and Rell. Plain and simple.

Before now, he had only suspected infidelity in their relationship. Now he was certain of it.

Chapter 14

The one-block stretch of Spaulding Avenue between Roosevelt Road and 13th Street was crawling with CPD officers. Among them were the homicide detectives assigned to investigate all of North Lawndale's gang-related murders: J.W. Bryant and Roy Milam.

There were two murder victims on the scene. One was a young black man with multiple gunshot wounds to the head, neck, and chest. He lay on the sidewalk with half of his inner organs in the snow-covered grass a couple of feet away. It was a horrific sight, one that would no doubt stick with every officer who'd seen the corpse before it was covered with a sheet.

The second body was a young black woman who had died in front of an apartment door. She'd taken a single .50-caliber round to the back. Judging from the position of her corpse, she had either been trying to twist the knob and enter the apartment to escape the shooters or knocking on the door for help. The young black couple inside the residence claimed to have no knowledge of who the victims were. Detective Milam had taken down their names before allowing them to leave, and now he and Bryant were standing over the male homicide victim. Bryant had the dead man's cell phone and was searching through it for clues.

"Didn't that girl look familiar to you?" Milam asked. He wore a white shirt, a blue tie, and gray slacks. A Marlboro cigarette was burning between his middle finger and forefinger, and his keen gray eyes were everywhere at once.

"Who?" Bryant said without looking up from the victim's phone. "You mean the vic on the stoop?"

"No. The girl from the apartment. She looks just like the girl we saw in the white Mercedes on Christmas Eve, the one you took the pics of on Drake Avenue."

Bryant looked up at Milam and smiled. "I ran the plates, remember? Yeah. Lakita Thomas was her name, and this one's name is *Tamia* Thomas. Think they're related?"

"They have to be related. They look too much alike *not* to be related."

"So Jahlil——"

"No, no, no. Let's forget about Jahlil Owens. He's a small fry." Milam took a hard pull on his Marlboro. "It's the guy who was in the passenger seat that we need to be looking at. The look in his eyes when he saw you snapping pictures of hi– that night - that said it all. And think about it: Jahlil Owens was shot right in front of that same Drake Avenue building. Then the guy from Michigan got it right across the street from there in the Christmas Day shooting that left that very same building peppered with bullet holes. The Michigan guy was found with an AK-47 next to his body, and since his brother was gunned down on Homan the night before Christmas, I think it's safe to assume he was there on a revenge mission. Two brazen shootouts at the same address within twenty-four hours? And then for us to have two –homas girls - who look like they could pass–for sisters - connected to all of this carnage is about as telling as any piece of evidence can be."

Bryant nodded, dropped the cell phone into an evidence bag, and said, "You may be onto something, because according to the texts in this phone, this guy's brothers are the Michigan brothers who were killed over the Christmas weekend." He gave the evidence bag to a passing officer and had another officer bring him the female victim's phone. Within seconds, he was smiling at his fellow detective.

"What is it?" Milam said anxiously.

"You're really a smart guy, you know that?" Bryant said, his navy blue CPD windbreaker rippling around him in the cold breeze.

"What is it?" Milam repeated.

"According to this call log, our dead girl's last conversation was with somebody named Tamia. And look at this." He showed Milam a picture in the phone's photo gallery. It was a selfie of the victim and Tamia smiling cheek to cheek beneath the glowing red sign that read REDBONE'S GENTLEMAN'S CLUB.

"I never believed it. That girl was high as shit. She was just saying something so she could leave."

"She was covering up for someone," Bryant said. "She knows our shooters."

"Of course she does." Milam flicked his cigarette into the dark sky as he and Bryant walked to Bryant's triple-black Dodge Challenger and got in.

"Hope you got some singles handy," Bryant said as he started the Hemi engine and lit his own Marlboro. "I'm willing to bet we'll find Tamia upside down inside of that strip club over on Trumbull."

"If it ain't white, it ain't right. Be damned if you have me in a club full of naked black whores. Not for any amount of time. We go in, arrest Tamia for obstruction, and take her down to the station for questioning. She'll break."

"Or we'll break *her*," Bryant said, driving off.

King Rio

Chapter 15

"Oh my God, baby, I had so much fun! I might have had one too many drinks, but I still had fun. We were celebrating the release of Oprah's new cookbook, and everybody was there."

Blake King looked up slowly. His brown eyes traveled over Alexus's porcelain-white flowy gown, from the fabric that pooled around her thick legs to the U-shaped opening of cleavage at her chest and finally to her gorgeous face and hypnotic green eyes. She was wearing her hair down, the right side swept back to display the flawless white diamonds dangling from the earlobe. She had just walked into his bedroom, regarded him with a fleeting glance (one too fleeting to realize that he was bent over the bed packing clothes into a suitcase) and dropped her eyes back down to the iPhone in her hand.

Blake's nostrils became wide and round like the holes at the business end of a double-barrel shotgun, and his platinum teeth slammed together. He was hit with a sudden realization: Meach was right. The Hennessy turned Blake into the man he'd been at eighteen, the corner-hustling, gun-slinging, fearless young goon who didn't give a fuck about anything.

"Tyler Perry was there," Alexus sailed on cheerfully. "Oprah, Gayle, Tika Sumpter, Beyoncé, most of the actors and actresses from –hows on OWN - we had a blast." Finally, she raised her eyes and looked at him long enough to see what he was doing. An expression of confusion replaced the joy on her face. One hand went to her hip, and she cocked her head to the side. "What's going on? Why are you packing?"

He didn't say anything, but he thought, *She's awfully happy for her two main bodyguards to have been killed thirty minutes ago.* He had three suitcases and two duffel bags already packed and zipped shut, and now he was zipping the fourth and last Louis Vuitton suitcase closed.

"Oh, so you can't hear? I thought we cleared the air in Dr. Farr's office earlier? Do you mean to tell me you're mad again?"

Blake snatched the suitcase off the bed and it hit the floor with a big thump. In the corner of his eye, he saw Alexus approaching him. There was a slit up the right leg of her gown that exposed her entire leg every time she brought that foot forward. She was roughly three feet away from him when he reached out and clamped his hand onto the front of her neck. In two great strides, he had her pinned against the wall next to the fireplace. Nose to nose, he glowered into her eyes.

Alexus held his gaze, a slight smile playing at her lips. Her eyes twinkled. She sniffed at the air between them. "Is that *liquor* I smell on your breath? I thought you quit drinking alcohol."

"You think this shit funny?" Blake said, and tightened his grip– on her neck - not enough to do any real harm, but enough to convey the level of seriousness he felt this shit deserved.

"What did I do now?" Alexus said. "Can I at least know what I'm being accused of? Innocent until p–oven guilty - ever heard of that?"

Blake responded not verbally but physically. He let go of her neck and used both hands to savagely rip the gown off of her. Piece by piece, he tore the gown to shreds and threw it to the marble floor. When he was done Alexus stood before him wearing nothing but her jewelry and her six-inch heels, and he found that somehow, in the midst of all that ripping and tearing, he had grown an erection.

"That's a forty-thousand dollar Atelier Versace gown you just destroyed," Alexus said tightly.

"Fuck you and that forty racks." This time he grabbed the back of her neck, walked her to the foot of his king-sized bed, and threw her head down onto the folded quilt that lay there across the bottom end of the heavy white comforter. With his free hand, he undid his belt and jeans.

"I didn't consent to this, Blake."

"Does it look like I give a fuck what you consented to?" He released his steel-hard phallus and began to wield it like a belt, striking her left buttock first and then striking her right one. His hard strikes made Alexus wince and reach back to shield her vulnerable derriere from the harsh whacks.

"Ouch! That hurts!" Alexus shrieked.

That was the point, Blake thought as he slid the head of his long fat sex muscle down to her vaginal opening and then rammed it in to the hilt, eliciting a sharp gasp from her. He moved his hand from the nape of her neck up to her hair, clenched a handful of it in his fist, and yanked her head back. Normally he worked up to a faster pace, but now he got right to it with long, hard thrusts.

He wasn't certain whether or not his intoxicated mind was playing tricks on him, but Alexus felt twice as wet as usual.

"You wanna get fucked, bitch? Huh?" Blake said, and there was an incredible amount of pent-up aggression in his voice. He took her hands, restrained them on her lower back, and continued his ruthless penile assault on her sopping-wet pussy.

Alexus whimpered and moaned beneath him like never before. He was pulling her hair so hard that her head was drawn all the way back, straining her neck.

"Apologize!" Blake barked the demand, and when Alexus didn't reply, he pushed his dick in as deep as it could go and forced a screaming moan from the depths of her soul. "Apologize *now!*"

"I'm… Mmm… mmm…sorry!"

"I know you're sorry; you didn't have to tell me that. I said *apologize.*" And in he went again, giving her about nine and a half of his ruler-sized member.

She screamed out a moan of the highest pitch. It was much louder than the steady smack-smack-smack of his pelvis beating against her ass.

"I…a-po-lo-gize," she said, with several of those opera-like moans between every spoken syllable.

"You dirty bitch." Blake let go of her hands and hair and shoved her down onto the bed. "Stay just like that, and don't move," he said as he took off every stitch of clothing he had on and tossed it all onto his brown leather suitcases.

He picked up a strip of fabric from the torn-to-pieces Versace gown and used it to tie her wrists together behind her back.

"You can't' fuck me that hard, Blake," she murmured weakly. "It hurts. It hurts my——"

He cut her off with another strip of expensive gown-fabric that he placed across her open mouth and tied around the back of her head. "I don't wanna hear that talk, you nasty bitch. You thing I'm stupid, but I'm *far* from stupid. You want some dick? I got dick for you. Like Kevin Hart said, bitch, you gon' learn what a big dick feels like today."

He snatched her up by"her 'air, turned her away from the bed, pushed her head forward, and entered her with one hard thrust. He fucked her savagely. The Hennessy played like a 100-milligram dose of Viagra in his bloodstream. He couldn't remember his dick ever being as hard as it was now. He let go of her hair, grabbed her hips, and went to work on her snugly-gripping pussy.

Blake looked around the massive bedroom. It was decorated in classic, high-end designer furniture. The art on the walls was expensive. This room was the master suite and featured a walk-in closet, dual-sinks, a Jacuzzi tub, and a pristine frameless glass shower with large televisions built into the two marble walls.

The sweet smell of Alexus's pussy filled the spacious room. Blake hooked an arm under her elbows and bent her over the bed again. She moaned and moaned and moaned.

"You wanted some dick, didn't you?" Blake was leaning over her, bellowing into her ear. "This what you wanted? Hmm? Is this what the fuck you wanted? If you got enough... energy to give another nigga some pussy...to give a nigga *my* pussy...then I ain't doing the job right. I'm about to fix that, though. That's what I'm about to do. Nuh-uh, where you going? Don't run now."

She was crawling up onto the bed, so he climbed on the bed right behind her, shoved her face down, and began to penetrate her with slow, deep strokes. And now he saw (and felt) why Alexus had –rawled away - she was having an orgasm. And intense one, by the feel of it. Her orgasmic fluids coated his dick and dripped down onto the bed. Her inner muscles contracted around him. He smacked her hard on the ass, and a grin appeared on his face.

"Hope you don't think it's over." He turned her over on her back, pushed her knees up to her ears, and sneered at her tear-filled eyes as he sank his dick into her slick sex. He wasted no time in returning to jackhammer speed. "You think I give a fuck about some tears? Bitch…" He slapped a hand onto the front of her neck like The Undertaker preparing to do a choke-slam and squeezed until green veins sprouted from her forehead.

Alexus had three more orgasms in the following fifteen minutes. Each time it happened, she tried to escape from beneath him, and each time he kept her captive, ramming his dick in and out of her with such powerful thrusts that she actually began to sob. The tears slipped from her eyes and trickled down into her ears. A perfect fusillade of moans climbed out of her throat. He kept his strong, veiny black hand locked on her neck, tightening and loosening, tightening and loosening, and when he felt himself on the verge of erupting, he choked her so hard her whole face turned red. He released his grip on her neck, pulled out of her, and stroked great ropes of semen onto her face while she gasped for breath.

"You happy now? Hmm?" The ejaculate was rushing out of him with the velocity of a firehose. "This what you wanted, right?" He nodded, as if answering for her.

The fiery anger he'd felt before the episode of rough sex diminished as his erection went flaccid. He untied her wrists. With trembling hands, she used the strips of torn fabric to mop the cum off her face as she sat up on the bed. He picked up a piece of fabric from the floor and wiped off his dick.

"You're so fucking mean," Alexus muttered.

"I believe," said Blake in a calm, measured voice, "that I'm a fair person. I only give people what they deserve."

"You tried to kill me." She rubbed her neck carefully. "Choked the fuck out of me. I could hardly even breathe."

"That was my intention," Blake said, with not the slightest trace of regret in his voice. "You didn't like it?"

She smiled. "I might not be able to walk right for the next few weeks, but I'd be a lie if I said I didn't enjoy that. You gotta start choking me more often."

"Really?" He reached for her neck.

"Not *now*!" Alexus knocked his hands away and laughed. "You know what I mean," she said, getting up. "During *sex*, you fucking psycho. Not for the hell of it."

She padded off into the bathroom, and Blake got dressed. He was fastening his belt when he consulted his inner thoughts and discovered that he had also enjoyed choking his wife during sex. Pulling her hair, too. He decided he'd do it again in the future, perhaps the next time he thought of her cheating on him with Rell.

Or with T-Walk.

Chapter 16

"What a house," Bubbles said.

"Especially from this angle." Juice looked up at the Villa Taj, the ten-million-dollar Burr Ridge estate where Bankroll Reese lived. They had just stopped out of the Maybach in front of the big whit mansion. Their family and friends were exiting other vehicles, and all of them were gawking in amazement at the towering white house. Bubbles had yet to stop smiling.

"From any angle," she suggested. "But I bet it looks even better on the inside." Bubbles reacted to his doubtful expression. "Worse?"

"You wouldn't think it was possible. I know. All Reese and his guys do is drink Lean and pop pills all day. He might've relied on the maids to fix up the place for this engagement dinner, but it's usually ugly in there."

"Let's hope it's not that way now."

They headed inside and were soon joined by their parents, siblings, and children. Juice's sister, Malaysia, had flown in from Nashville with her three children. Bubbles had her sister, Kisha, and their mother, along with her daughter, Ra'Mya. Her mother and Juice's mother were already chatting it up as everyone flooded into a dining room with two long tables that were covered with dishes of soul food: greens, fried chicken, mac and cheese, and a hundred other delicious choices. There was seating for eighteen at each table, but hardly anyone sat. Not when there was music, fun games, and endless drinks in the ballroom.

Dawn and Wayno had made it in. Juice's ex-wife, Shakela, was also in the house. She sat at a table with Rose, Bankroll Reese's mom, at the opposite side of the ballroom from where Juice and Bubbles sat. Shawnna and Reese took the table to the left of Bubbles and Juice, along with Wayno and Dawn. Jennifer Hudson's soulful voice wailed out from speakers overhead and kept the room lively.

"And you claim my place is big," Bubbles said, beaming.

"It is," Juice said, with a smile that matched hers.

"This big-ass mansion makes my house look like your little-ass apartment you got on Drake."

"That's why I live with you now."

Lakita Thomas sat and looked at him. As a social media sex symbol, she often dressed as if to outdo every big-bootied model on the web a hundredfold for even attempting to complete with her. Tonight was no exception. Juice smiled at what Bubbles had considered the right thing to wear for this occasion, an evening of entertaining their closest loved ones and celebrating their engagement. They had detoured to her Lake Forest home for her to change clothes before coming here. Her long, thick legs were wrapped in a snug, see-through white dress slashed with hot-pink stripes. Not many women could handle the illusion of width such a horizontal pattern projected across the posterior, but Lakita Thomas, thick as a Snicker, managed to look stunning. The cropped top of the dress exposed a lovely midriff. A bevy of sparkling white diamonds glittered in her Tiffany earrings, Chanel necklace, LeVian tennis bracelets, and the Ritani engagement ring on her most special finger. In this dazzling outfit, more suited, perhaps, for a stripper convention at Redbone's Gentleman's Club than a family affair, Bubbles began snapping pictures of the ring with her iPhone, angling the eye of the camera this way and that way, smiling ceaselessly. "You really surprised me with this, Juice. I mean, like, *really* surprised me."

"I know."

"What made you do it?"

Juice had asked himself the same question a hundred times since he'd purchased the ring two days ago. "Maybe because you're the realest woman I've ever been with, and I didn't wanna let one fucked up marriage discourage me from giving you what you truly deserve."

"I'm giving you what *you* deserve for *this*," Bubbles said.

"What's that supposed to mean?"

"You'll find out tonight."

"In that case, I'll be sure to stay up.–*All* the way - like Remy Ma and Fat Joe."

Bubbles sat back in her chair and laughed. "Y'all got me so good. Had me thinking Kisha was taking Ra'Mya to see a movie. Had me wondering where my mom was all day..."

"I know, I know." All of today's surprises had been stressful in the making, but the end results made the secretive planning all the more worth it.

They looked at each other. Her blond-dyed hair fell over her pronounced forehead in long straight bangs, while the rest hung around her head in a neatly-slanted bob. "So is it okay if I pick a date for the wedding now, or do you want to wait?"

"That's up to you, baby. I mean...well, not *now*. We can take us a two-week cruise to Mexico or something. I say we wait for summer to tie the knot."

"Nuh-uh. Mexico's off the list. I just read an article on CNNs website about thirty-two dead bodies that were found in a meat-packing factory in Mexico just yesterday. Thirty of the bodies were cut in half from top to bottom, and one was found with his head stuck up a cow's ass. I ain't fucking with those Mexicans."

The mention of Mexicans brought the text message he'd received from Bulletface to the front of Juice's mind. He told Bubbles about it, and her eyes got wide.

"How'd he find...oh, never mind. I know how he found out," she said, and shook her head.

"Who told him?"

"You might as well say I did. I told Tasia about it, and she told him as soon as he called her."

Juice shrugged. "Fuck it. I got a thousand bricks out the deal, and I ain't paid him a dime yet. If he wanna get mad about the shit, I'll pull a Plies in a heartbeat."

"Run off on the plug?"

"Twice," Juice said, and they both laughed.

"You are so crazy."

"I'm just playing," he said. Denial was his friend. "I wouldn't run off with ten million dollars of tax-free money from a nigga I hardly even know. That would be ungrateful. You know I'm better than that." His smile said otherwise.

The fact was, Juice had been selling drugs for a very long time, everything from grams and eight-balls to ounces and nine-pieces, but now he was in the major league. He'd sold almost five hundred kilograms of uncut cocaine in less than a week, most of them to men who'd messaged and called the Google smartphone Bulletface gave him when they agreed to the 1,000-kilogram deal. Bulletface had promised to send some clientele his way, but he hadn't expected so many kilos to be sold so soon. After only a couple of days as a drug kingpin, vicariously connected to half a dozen murders and under surveillance by the CPD (or at least the CPD homicide detectives who'd snapped a photo of him on Christmas Eve), Juice had already lost his bearings. How had he come to accept all the craziness? Perhaps it was the pace at which the kilograms sold, and the intensity. It kept him dizzy enough to begin to doubt if up was up and down was down.

"Set the date for this coming up July," he said to the one person whose presence kept him together through all the insanity. "That'll give us enough time to se– everything - no, I ta–e that back - it'll give *you* enough time to set everything up. I'm not getting involved in the wedding plans."

"Why not? And don't say it's because you're a man," Bubble said, scrolling through the photos she'd just taken of her ring. She selected one and began the arduous task of posting it to Instagram.

"Then I won't say it."

"You don't care about what goes on at our wedding?"

"Nope."

Bubbles rolled her eyes, captioned the photo. *#Taken*, added the diamond ring and heart-eyed emojis, and uploaded the photo to her Instagram page for all of her nearly three million followers to see. "What about our honeymoon?" she continued. "Or is that also out of your range?"

"Naaah, now you're talking my language," Juice said, grinning. He would have said more if her twelve-year-old daughter hadn't popped up between them at the very moment.

"Big Nasty," Ra'Mya said, smiling her mother's smile. She planted an elbow on Juice's shoulder. "Is it okay if I stick to calling you Big Nasty? After you and my momma get married, is what I mean."

"Who made it okay to begin with?" Juice asked, but Ra'Mya was cheek to cheek with Bubbles, smiling for an Instagram photo Bubbles was getting ready to take.

#Twinsies

Juice got up to work the crowd. Shawnna and Dawn were standing close together on one side of their table, while Bankroll Reese stood with his squad of Lean-sipping gang members at the other side. The livid expression on Dawn's face was palpable. Juice walked up behind both of his beautiful young daughters and draped his arms around their shoulders. "What's going on?" he said, looking at Dawn.

"She's mad about that Snapchat video," Shawnna said. "Even though she ain't been with Cage in God knows how long, she's mad that he went and hooked up with the queen of all thots. I don't know *why* she's still in love with that ugly-ass nigga."

Juice gave Shawnna a stern look, which, thanks to many long years of practice, she quite easily ignored. "Oh my God, Daddy. Can you believe I'm actually engaged now? We're getting married on Valentine's Day of twenty-eighteen. That'll give me a whole year to get all our wedding plans in order, and that's more than enough time to lose the weight I put on with this baby in my stomach."

"Y'all could've waited for me to get her before y'all proposed," Dawn said bitterly. She had her arms folded across her chest, her lower lip thrust out in a seething pout. Juice gave her a kiss on the temple and a rub on the shoulder, hoping to calm her, but the anger in her eyes stood its ground. "Tamia did that because I went to Jamaica with Wayno. She got pissed off about it and went after Cage to get me back, and his dumb ass fell for it. Ugh, I could just kill him right now. Gon' let that girl put her mouth on him after she done put her mouth on every nigga in the neighborhood."

"You should've put *your* mouth on him," Shawnna suggested.

"I'm not putting my mouth on *no* damn body," Dawn countered, and Juice took this as his cue to walk around the circular wooden table to join his nephew Kev and Bankroll Reese.

"Man, I'm telling you," Reese was saying, "the nigga came out of nowhere with the K and started bussin'. We would've been hit up if one of 'em hadn't accidentally let a shot off before they got close enough to us…"

Reese was describing the Christmas Day shooting. He and his bodyguard Chubb had been there, as well as Wayno and the twins. Juice had heard the story a hundred times from Dawn and Shawnna.

He glanced down into the Styrofoam cups Reese and Kev were sipping from, saw cubes of ice floating around in purple liquid, and shook his head disappointedly.

"You niggas need to go to rehab," Juice said, and shook his head.

"Man, we ain't even got started yet." Reese sipped some of his narcotic beverage and said, "I flew in some of the baddest bitches from all over the country, big homie. I got Roc from Trap House in New York, Skittles from Zamba Rio in Brooklyn, Chela and Vanity from Purlieu nightclub in New York. You know I'm a lifelong stripper connoisseur. I got this bitch that danced at Pure Passion West in Indianapolis for the party, too. Her nam–'s Nastasha - can't remember he– stage name - but the bitch got ass like Bubbles." He cut a glance at Juice. "No disrespect, big homie. I'm just saying. We got some bad bitches on the way. You might as well call tonight our first official bachelor party, 'cause it's crackin'."

"Where exactly is all this supposed to be taking place?" Juice asked.

"Where else?" Reese said. "Redbone's."

Chapter 17

Night came on in Michigan City and the stars unrolled across the sky from east to west like a black blanket with spangle in it. The wind blew light sprays of snow across the road and whistled around Rell's Benz as he steered it northbound on Franklin Street behind his brother's Benz, which Tirzah was driving, with Tamera and the Cartwright sisters as passengers. Tirzah was a careful driver, despite her freewheeling ways in other pursuits, and she obeyed the speed limit as she led the way to Club Manna's. In the glare from the halogen street lamps overhead, the two sleek Mercedes Benzes cruised along at a steady thirty-five, enjoying the 9:00 p.m. treat of minimal traffic.

The big blob of a man that was Lil Phil sat in the passenger seat next to Rell, eating out of a large bag of bite-size Snickers bars he'd extracted from somewhere inside his coat, breathing the way Darth Vader had when he revealed that he had broken his lightsaber off in Luke Skywalker's mother. He had been climbing into his Dodge Durango when Rell offered him a ride in the Benz, a ride he had gladly accepted. Offering Lil Phil a ride was the least Rell could do. After all, the fat man had essentially offered Rell his father on a silver platter.

"You ever been to Nap Town?" Lil Phil asked, looking at Rell's profile as they passed a liquor store and an Al's Supermarket, the passing streetlights flooding the car interior with pulses of light and dark.

"Nah, I ain't left Chicago since I was born."

"I was just in Chir–q last week - ain't that what they call it now?"

Lil Phil nodded; his jowls quaked. "I understand what you mean. That's what the young, dumb niggas call it, huh? Same as in my city. They done started calling it Napghanistan. Some coward shit, really. Niggas scared to get beat up. We used to throw hands all the time. At the club,–at the rink - all we did was fight."

"You said you was in Chicago last week?" Rell asked, digging for more information.

"Yeah, but only for a day. Some nigga killed my cousin Jamal. We went looking for the nigga on the night before Christmas Eve. My cousin Mila told us to look for a black Escalade, that's the truck we went looking for. We drove back and f–rth through - what side you from?"

"I'm from the south side," Rell lied.

"We went through the west side looking for that Escalade, up and down 16th Street. Then we heard about twenty gunshots, and I told my pops to get us the fuck up outta there. It's crazy too, 'cause we drove right past the body. He was a big nigga, about my size. Looked like he got ran off the road, or it might've been accidental. They had a snowstorm that night, a real bad one, and we damn near went off the road a few times ourselves. Whatever the case, the nigga got shot up right there on the sidewalk, about ten feet from his van. I know the van was his 'cause I looked up the murder on the Internet the next day. His name was Christopher Walsh."

Rell knitted his brows together and shook his head. "Never heard of him," he said, although he had known Christopher Walsh, alias Styro, for quite a long time. The black Escalade they'd been searching for was currently parked in front of Rell and Tamera's redbrick bungalow home on the west side of Chicago. It had belonged to his late father.

"Anyway, though," Lil Phil continued, tearing open his umpteenth mini Snickers, "Pops brought me and my li'l brother back out here. We kicked it with Keyanna that night, and Pops went back to Chicago. Only reason I remember what day it was is 'cause I'm the one who took the eviction notice off Krystal's door that night. Pops caught the nigga in Chicago that next morning. That's when his truck got shot up."

Eviction notice? Despite Rell's ravenous hunger for every morsel of information pertaining to his brother being shot four days ago, the mention of Krystal's eviction notice struck a chord in his heart. Rell had been raised by a single–black woman - his m–ther, Maria - and, during his stint in prison, he'd read books on Assaata Shakur, Angelo Davis, Ida B. Wells, Susan B. Anthony, and also Michael Eric Dyson's *Why I Love Black Women*. He had a soft spot in his heart for the plight of African American women, and he couldn't help feeling for Krystal.

"So she's getting evicted?" he said, and lit his fourteenth Newport of the day.

"She gotta be out by January twenty-fourth," Lil Phil said, nodding his neck-less head. "They gave her thirty days."

"For what?"

"Noise complaints, police calls, unpaid rent. It's not really her fault. Her and Keyanna got some haters. Bitches be calling the police every chance they get. Krystal makes enough to pay the bills, but she also takes care of Keyanna most of the time, and their other sister's kids in Flint."

"So she got two sisters?"

Lil Phil gave another head-jiggling nod. "Kenyetta is the oldest sister. She's in the Feds. I guess her boyfriend was a kingpin in Detroit. She got caught up in the indictments a few years ago. Her kids are in jail too."

"Damn. How old are the kids?"

"You gotta ask Krystal. I know they ain't grown, because they're both in juvenile jails. The nephew got caught with a gun and some dope in his locker at school, and the niece got arrested for beating up the girl who snitched on her brother. She beat the girl with one of those big combination locks. Judge gave her eighteen mont's in a girls' school. Both of 'em coming to stay with Krystal when they get out."

"If she has a place to stay," Rell commented. His brows were drawn together again, because Tirzah was turning into the entrance of a Rally's restaurant parking lot. It wasn't until he eased into the parking space beside hers that he realized how hungry he was.

"Nigga," Lil Phil said, suddenly bursting with excitement, "you ever ate a spicy chicken sandwich from here?"

Rell shook his head no.

"*What*! Are you fuckin' *serious*? Lil Phil shoved open his door, put the large Snickers bag back inside of his coat, and hurriedly lifted himself out of the car. "Wait until you taste this sandwich, bro. On the hood."

Phil and the Cartwright sisters walked abreast toward the restaurant, with Tirzah right behind them.

"Hold on, baby," Rell said to Tamera, taking her arm above the elbow. He gave the others a smile that felt as genuine as a seven-dollar bill. "We'll be in as soon as I finish this cigarette." He guided Tamera over to the rear end of his car, looking back over his shoulder at the fat man three or four times as he did. It didn't seem like a good idea to turn his back on Lil Phil completely.

Leaning her hip against the shiny silver lettering that declared his car to be an S550, Tamera said, "I need my phone back to lock in Krystal's number. I know what we're here for, but can it wait until tomorrow? I am having so much fun out——"

She shut her mouth abruptly as her eyes fell upon the two iPhones Rell had just pulled from the left-hand pocket of his expensive sweatpants. He turned one of them over so she could see the clear piece of Scotch tape and the sticky fragments of chewing gum on the back. She gasped when she saw it.

"That's your phone!" Tamera shrieked.

"*Shhh*! The hell is wrong with you? Quiet down," Rell admonished.

"My bad," she said, whispering now, the warmth of her breath creating smoke in the cold night air between them. "How did you get it back?"

"Phil had it. His pops is the one who shot Jah."

"*What*?" Tamera seemed to be just as shocked by the news that the fat man's father had tried to kill Jah as the fat man had been when Rell told him he'd never tasted a Rally's spicy chicken sandwich. She took the phone and studied it closely. "Well, I'll be damned. So the man we just bought our loud from is related to the man who tried to kill my brother-in-law."

"He told me the whole story. He was in the hood with his pops looking for my Escalade when Styro got whacked. Mila told them to look for the black Escalade."

"Y'all should've never picked that bitch up in your truck."

"Don't blame me."

"It's just as much your fault as it is Jah's."

The Brick Man 5

"Whatever. His pops is coming to the club we're going to. I told him I know a guy who owns a car lot, somebody his pops can get a new pickup truck from for cheap, so I'm supposed to be meeting his pops at the club when we get there." He took one last drag of his cigarette and then pitched it to the ground and watched as the wind carried it away. "Stay on point. No more drinks tonight."

"Okay," Tamera said. "Are you planning on trying to bring your gun in with you? You know they'll probably have metal detectors."

"I'll leave it in the car. Hopefully I won't need it until I leave out."

"Whatever you do," she warned, "don't drink anything Lil Phil drinks out of. He slipped something in Krystal's drink a few months ago and raped her."

"He just told me that."

"Sick fuck," Tamera said glumly.

"It's all good. He'll get what's coming to him." Rell gave her the phone with the tape and chewing gum residue on it. "You know the code. Same as always. Two-zero-two-two-one-two. You use my phone and I'll use yours. As of now he thinks I bought the phone from his for the fuck of it, so don't pull it out at the club. Not if he's anywhere near you."

Tamera slipped the phone into the rear right-side pocket of her jeans, leaned toward him, and kissed him on the mouth. Her tongue ventured out as it always did after she'd ingested hard liquor. She smiled around the kiss, then drew herself back. "Sincere Jerrell Owens."

"The realest nigga you'll ever meet."

"Don't do anything stupid when we get to the club. I'm not trying to lose my husband before we even get to celebrate our first anniversary of marriage."

"I'm the sober one, remember?"

"I know. I know." She sighed and shook her head. "When this night comes to an end, it better be me and you in the bed doing some seriously X-rated things to each other."

"I wouldn't have it any other way," Rell said, and this time it was him who did the kissing.

Chapter 18

Trintino Walkson steered his rented 2016 Lamborghini Aventador Roadster into the alleyway behind Manna's and pulled up to the back door of the nightclub. A Bentley Flying Spur came to a stop behind the Lamborghini, followed by a Ferrari 458 Italia. All three of the luxury vehicles were painted blue, albeit in different shades. The four men in the Bentley were Gangster Disciples. They were also members of Trintino Walkson's old crew, TSH, short for Tenth Street Hustlers. The two men in the Ferrari were also Gangster Disciples, though they were from the southside of Chicago.

"I have a bad feeling about this," Ashley Hunter said fearfully. She was next to T-Walk in the passenger seat, wrapped in a full-length blue fur coat. Her hair was dyed blue at the edges. Her fingernails and toenails were blue-tipped, her lipstick was blue, and the Prada jumpsuit she wore under the coat was also blue. "The last time we were here together, Alexus put a gun to my head and then killed your guys in that office. Then you and Blake almost killed each other right here in this alley."

T-Walk nodded his head solemnly. He remembered that night vividly, but he wasn't going to allow that dark memory to deter him from making a triumphant return to his city.

And make no mistake about it, this was most definitely T-Walk's city.

True enough, Blake King was the most successful person to ever come from Michigan City, Indiana. He was a certified goon, a real street nigga who had sold crack-rocks on the west side of town with his crew, the Dub Life Goons, before meeting his current wife and rising to fame as Bulletface the rapper. But T-Walk was the man who'd supplied Blake and most of the other drug dealers with cocaine back then. Most of the gang members in this city were Gangster Disciples, and T-Walk was by far the most respected and honored GD in the entire state. Here on the east –ide of town - commonly referred to–as Eastport - Trintino "T-Walk" Walkson was king.

He donned a light-blue three-piece Gucci suit and a Rolex wristwatch that had blue diamond encrusted all throughout its bezel and band. "Let's not dwell on the past," he said, his tone of voice brimming with confidence. He took Ashley's hand in his and squeezed it firmly. "And besides, when I owned this club, it was operated by nothing but gang members and dope boys. Everything's professional now. Look at the security."

Ashley Hunter, known to reality TV watchers as Thunder, the full-figured Nigerian-American who had gone from dating a Miami Heat star on *Basketball Wives* to being T-Walk's leading lady for the ninth or tenth time, had already checked out the security. There were four police officers at the opening of the alley where they had entered after the two MCPD squad cars blocking it nose to nose had momentarily separated to let them in. The other end of the alleyway appeared to be just as secure as the former end. Another cop was currently walking past the nightclub's back door. He was strolling back down the length of the alleyway. His shadow grew long, shortened in the glow of the hanging fluorescents, then grew long again.

"I know we're safe," Ashley said. "It's just a memory, you know? Especially after Alexus had me dangled over the balcony of a New York high-rise and held captive in an abandoned factory warehouse. I still haven't gotten over that. I get chills every time I think about it."

"But didn't I come and save you from those Mexicans?"

"Yeah," she said wanly, "but it still happened. I still have a knot on the back of my head."

"That should make you feel even better every time we spend a dollar of the ten million dollars I got out of them. Not to mention all the millions we're about to get from them for the rights to my story."

"I wish our plan to break them up with the release of that picture of you hugging her would have worked."

"It did work."

"How'd it work if TMZ's reporting that they reunited after a marriage counseling session with some celebrity shrink in West Hollywood?"

"It worked because that picture broke them up to begin with," T-Walk said. "Their marriage is weak now. They'll both be walking on eggshells, doing everything in their power not to piss the other one off. It won't be long before one of them fucks up. Then Alexus will be single and mine for the taking."

Ashley whipped her head around and scowled at him. *"Come again?"*

"Not like that," he laughed. 'I'm talking about her money. I'll be able to get at least $200 million out of her with Blake gone. I didn't mean it like me and her getting back together. That'll never happen."

"It better not."

"It won't." He gave her hand another reassuring squeeze, packed her on the cheek, and picked up his smartphone.

He was lying about not wanting to get back with Alexus. What man in his right mind *wouldn't* want to get with Alexus? Hell, what *woman* wouldn't want to get with Alexus Costilla? She was the baddest chick in the game, hands down. And her eleven-figure net worth made her even more appealing.

T-Walk was just about to dial the club owner's phone number when the nightclub's back door swung open. It was Michael Manna, and he led T-Walk and the gang inside. As soon as they entered the back door, T-Walk heard the incessant chant of "T-Walk's Back!" being shouted over the bass of Rae Sremmurd's "Black Beatles."

"They're going crazy for you out there," Michael said, handing T-Walk a cash-filled envelope. "That's the whole ten racks, just like we discussed. Bottles on me. You just enjoy yourself in VIP with your crew. I got you personal security, hot wings, big bottles of Moet and Chandon."

"How many people in here?" T-Walk asked as they traversed a stone-walled hallway that led to the VIP room.

"Almost two thousand people, I believe. A lot of them came from Gary, South Bend, Chicago, East Chic–go, Hammond - you got a lot of fans. And of course you know most of the street niggas you rocked with came to show love. It's a celebration."

They came to a fogged-glass door with a camera mounted over it, and Michael Manna stopped everyone. Ashley had her iPhone ready to record video of T-Walk's entrance for the millions of people that followed him on Snapchat and Instagram. The roar of "T-Walk's Back" went on and on beyond the door. T-Walk felt his heart drumming in his chest.

"You ready?" the club owner asked T-Walk.

"Yeah."

"Before we go in, I have to tell you one thing. Only because I know you didn't get along well with certain guys in the past, certain cliques, and I don't want any trouble to arise, you know what I mean?" Michael Manna had a nervous look on his dark-hued face. "Do you know Young Meach? Dub Life Young Meach, the one signed with Money Bagz?"

"Yeah," T-Walk said. "Why?"

"Because he's here."

"That ain't a problem. Meach used to work for me back in the day. As far as I'm concerned, all that old beef is squashed, fam. I'm on a paper chase."

Michael nodded and opened the door.

Cameras flashed like strobe lights as T-Walk made his entrance. The VIP section was merely an elevated hardwood platform at the back of the club. It was sectioned off by a four-feet-high wall and had just eight tables. There were hundreds of men and women crowded shoulder to shoulder with their smartphones aimed at T-Walk. The majority of the faces were African-American, and all of them were smiling. He saw his face on a lot of T-shirts.

Two VIP tables were already taken. Meach and four more guys were at one table, while a fat guy, an average-sized guy in a hoodie, and four stunningly beautiful young women occupied the other table. They all stood and applauded as T-Walk went to the short wall and greeted a few dozen people with handshakes and hugs. Jeezy's "Put On" began to throb through the club's big speakers. Girls T-Walk hadn't seen in years planted kisses on his face. It was a lot to deal with, and he was glad to finally turn around and go to his table a moment later.

As soon as he sat down, Ashely leaned in and whispered in his ear. "Alexus must have sent her little girl squad to stalk you."

"What are you talking about?" T-Walk said, studying the crowd.

"The girls at the other VIP table. Two of them were in those pictures with Alexus and Blake. See?" Ashley showed him the photo Alexus had posted on Instagram last week, and sure enough, two of the girls were the same girls that were seated three tables away.

T-Walk smiled and waved at the girls. He remembered seeing them eating dinner with Alexus at Papi's, her Hollywood restaurant. It was obvious by the looks on their faces that they also remembered him. Looking at them now, he felt almost certain that they were sisters. Their identical noses, high cheekbones, and similar blond hairstyles gave them away.

His attention shifted to a line of sexy young women that had just begun to saunter into the VIP section. They were holding large bottles of Moet champagne out in front of them. Sparklers attached to the bottles sizzled brightly. T-Walk invited the girls from the other table over to drink with him, but only three of them joined him. The dark-skinned girl stayed in her seat. Her sister ran up to T-Walk and excitedly introduced herself.

"Hey, T-Walk! I'm not sure if you remember me or not but my name is Tirzah and I saw you this past Friday at——"

"Papi's," he finished for her. "I remember."

Tirzah pointed over her shoulder at the dark-skinned girl. "That's my li'l sister, Tamera. She was there too."

"I remember," T-Walk repeated, pulling out his phone as it started ringing with a call from a close female friend of his. He held up a forefinger to Tirzah and the others and went back out to the hallway. He pulled the door shut and answered the call. "What up, sis?"

"Bro," Tasia "Baddie Barbie" Olsen said, "why the hell haven't you been answering your phone? This is my fifth time calling you in the past two days."

"Been busy, fam."

"I've been trying to let you in on something I found out about your ex-girlfriend," Barbie said, and there was a conspiratorial tone to her soft voice.

The hallway was long and relatively narrow. There were cameras on the ceiling and it was bright enough in spite of the gray, clean brick walls. T-Walk leaned back against the wall. "What is it? You gotta hurry up. I'm at a paid club event in Michigan City."

"How far is that from Chica–o?"

"It's - wait, you in Chicago?"

"Mm-hmm."

"It's about a forty-minute drive," he said, glancing at the door. "You got five seconds, fam."

"Alexus cheated on Blake with a married couple last week. It happened backstage at the D-Boy and Deja concert at the Staples Center last week. The man's name was –ell or Real - something like that. The woman's name was Tamera. They had a threesome."

T-Walk's mouth and eyes widened involuntarily and he gaped at the bricks on the wall across from him for a long moment. Barbie read his silence correctly.

"I know, right?" she said. "Shocked the hell out of me too. And I know for a fact it's true, because my girl was there when it went down that night. Her, her fiancé, and the Tamera g–rl's sister - all three of 'em was in that dressing room."

A slow smile crept across the bottom of T-Walk's face. It grew until the corners of his mouth felt as if they were approaching the lobes of his ears. Dear Jesus, why was Alexus making this so easy for him?

"Answer this question, and then I gotta go," he said. "The Tamera g–rl's sister - her name wouldn't happen to be Tirzah, would it?"

Barbie gasped. "How'd you know that?"

"I'll hit you back." T-Walk ended the call abruptly and headed back into the VIP room with the huge smile still pasted on his face.

Chapter 19

Tamia had mastered the art of dancing like a stripper way back in middle school. She knew how to make her ass clap. She knew how to bounce her ass while doing the splits. In fact, she could perform better than most of the veteran strippers she danced with at Redbone's Gentleman's Club. Which is why she wasn't the least bit worried about competing with the twelve out-of-town girls that had walked into the locker room a short while ago.

All the girls were lined up in front of the wall-to-wall mirror, glamming up for the stage. Candy, one of the only two dancers Tamia had befriended, was sitting on the leather-padded stool next to Tamia's. She popped her head over into Tamia's space. "Hey…Shortcakes. You got a minute?"

"Sure. What's up?" Tamia said, and chuckled once. She was still getting used to being called Shortcakes. Bankroll Reese had given her the name after watching her audition video.

"I'm so ready to break down and cry right now, Tamia. I mean, I am sick. Chandra is really dead. I can't believe that shit."

"Keep it together, bitch. Don't let these hoes see you crying. Believe me, I'm just as fucked up about it as you are, if not more. It happened on my doorstep."

Candy began to tear up. She was a lean and narrow-headed girl who reminded Tamia of Rihanna. The yellow-brown Chicago version. She was, according to Bubbles, one of the "real bitches" who stripped at Redbone's.

Tamia picked up her box of Kleenex tissue and offered it to Candy. She took three, one-two-three, and wadded them into a pink ball and wiped her eyes.

"I wish I could say I had known that Marshall was going to get shot at on sight," Tamia said, "but I haven't talked to Wayno ever since he went to Jamaica. He's the one who always keeps me in the loop about what's going on in the streets."

"I don't know how you didn't know when we just talked about it last night."

"Bitch, I was drunk. I can barely even remember going home. And will you please stop crying before you get me started?" Tamia was carefully applying a second coat of Covergirl So Lashy! Mascara to her eyelashes, trying her best not to think about Chandra, Marshall, and the two homicide detectives she and Cage had encountered as they left her apartment.

Candy began giggling through her tears, sitting beside Tamia in the brightly-lit locker room. The girl on the other side of Tamia was one of the out-of-towners. She had SKIDDLEZ tattooed across the top of her back, and Tamia thought she was one of the most beautiful women in the world, a yellow bitch with long curly red hair and a bunch of colorful tattoos all over her sexy body.

"You ain't shit for that Snapchat sex with Cage," Candy said, shaking her head. "I spit out a mouthful of Fruit Loops when I first saw it. Me and my main nigga watched it about twenty times in a row."

"I don't see why Dawn broke up with him, to tell you the truth. He got a good dick game."

"You know she's back from Jamaica, right?"

Tamia looked at Candy in the mirror. "Really?"

"On my brother's grave. She's at Bankroll Reese's mansion right now. Oh my God, have you *seen* his mansion? Shawnna is so fucking lucky. Not only is she pregnant by Bankroll Reese, but now she's actually *engaged* to Bankroll Reese. She might as well just retire now, because she's pretty much set for life."

"Do you think Reese will fire me if Dawn and Shawnna asked him to?"

"I don't... Hmm. Good question. I'd hope not." Candy paused and stared at her iPhone. "Just keep it cute. If you're gonna fuck with Cage then do your thing, but don't go tweeting at Dawn or sending shots at her on the Gram. Remember where you're getting money from. You know the saying: never shit where you eat. Offending Dawn puts your toilet a little too close to your dinner table, if you get my drift."

Tamia nodded. "I definitely get it," she said. No matter how good Cage's dick game was, it wasn't worth jeopardizing her cash flow.

"She'll more than likely be here tonight with Reese and Shawnna. They should be walking in any minute now," Candy said, and was that a tone of trepidation she was speaking with? It certainly sounded like one to Tamia.

"Don't let them bitches jump me like they did Chandra," Tamia said, looking and feeling worried. "I know my cousin ain't about to let me get beat up, but your ass better be there to help if they try it."

"What you need to do is call Bubbles and talk to her before they get here. That way you can clear the air before it comes to blows."

"Are you going to help me if they jump me?" Tamia said, emphasizing every word.

Candy replied in the same manner. "No, I will not help you. Not if helping you means fighting my boss's new fiancée or her sister. I make good money working here. And let's not forget that Shawnna is like Laila Ali out in these streets. If that bitch ever swings on me, I'm running for a weapon. Fuck that shit. Not about to get my ass beat." She gave Tamia a pat on the shoulder as she got up from her stool. "You're on your own with this one, Shortcakes."

She smacked Tamia on the ass and then went sauntering out of the locker room, her big fake butt bouncing like two basketballs on an invisible floor. Tamia offered her a middle finger. Skittles smiled and turned to Tamia, who was getting ready to FaceTime Bubbles.

"I don't mean to get in your business," Skittles said, "but did I just hear her say you need to call Bubbles? As in the same Bubbles who used to be with Bulletface?"

Tamia nodded. "She's my cousin."

It was as if a huge balloon of excitement suddenly burst open in the red-haired girl's chest. Her eyes went wide, her mouth fell agape, and she gasped. "You look like her too! I *love* her! We were just talking about her on the way here! She's the baddest stripper ever. We were saying earlier this year that Blacc Chyna was the queen of strippers for the move she pulled with Rob, but Bubbles actually fucked Bulletface. Not only that, but she also made Alexus so jealous over a simple picture that Alexus tried to kill Bulletface over it. Compare all you want, but you can't go any higher than Blake King. You just can't. It's impossible. Bulletface went from being the king of the Midwest to the king of the whole rap games, and he's still the finest nigga to ever do it."

"You ain't *never* lied," Tamia said excitedly. She high-fived the girl and then FaceTimed her cousin, while many of the girls began to file out of the locker room.

It was time for all of them to get to work. Someone shouted that Jimmy Butler and another Bulls player had just entered the building, and that a few dope boys with deep pockets were planning on coming through some time tonight.

When Bubbles answered, Tamia saw that she was standing in a room full of people, presumably inside of Bankroll Reese's mansion. There was a benevolent glow to Bubbles that swelled Tamia's heart with a searing warmth of happiness. Bubbles immediately raised her left hand to show off her engagement ring.

"I absolutely cannot stand you," Tamia said, smiling.

"You're not the only one feeling that way tonight."

"Juice's ex-wife must be there."

"Mm-hmm. The past Mrs. Wilkins is in the same room with the future Mrs. Wilkins. It's not how you'd think it would be. She actually congratulated me and him. I think Dawn told her to do it, though."

"I was calling to talk to you about Dawn."

"Just talk to her when we get there. We'll be heading out in a couple of minutes."

Tamia squinted at Bubbles. It was funny because the squint was Bubbles' signature expression.

"Don't play with me, Lakita. I'm not about to be in here fighting over Cage's ugly ass."

"Do you think I'd just sit back and let somebody hurt you?"

"I ain't worried about nobody hurting me," Tamia lied, and blew out a great sigh of relief. "Girl, tell me why Chandra got killed right outside my apartment door."

"Lil Mark called and told Juice about that a few hours ago. Luke's son got hit in the stomach, too."

"Ain't tha' sad?"

"Li'l cous, ain't nothing sad to me tonight. Kev said he had just told Juice that he thought Chandra might've been involved in that Christmas shooting. She swore up and down she didn't know they were going to do it, that she hadn't heard from Marshall ever since that day, and that she would let Juice know if she heard from him again, but look who she was with."

Tamia nodded her head somberly. "Marshall was her boy-friend."

"That's none of my business. Karma's a bitch in red-bottoms, though. I know that much. What I need for you to do is stay out of the drama. Keep your mind on the money and nothing else. Now let me go."

"Love you, big cousin," Tamia chirped.

"Bitch, I hate you too," Bubbles said, still glowing with that special kind of joy only a marriage proposal can bring. "See you when I get there."

For a moment Tamia sat there on the stool and gazed at her reflection in the mirror. Her pupils were dilated from the X pills she'd ingested, and her body was full of energy. She stood up, gave herself a once-over, then put her purse and phone in her locker and went out to work the floor.

King Rio

Chapter 20

For a six-person table in the VIP section at Manna's, the regular price was $125. T-Walk's appearance jacked the price up 400%, but Rell didn't mind the five-hundred-dollar price tag, especially since Lil Phil had gone half with him on the ticket. Now every table was taken. T-Walk and his gang occupied four tables, and Young Meach had bought up the last two, though there were several open seats at those tables.

Tirzah had yet to leave T-Walk's side. Krystal and Keyanna kept going from table to table, smoking hookahs and drinking liquor. Keyanna seemed more interested in Meach and his crew, and Rell understood why. Meach was practically dripping in diamonds. He was one of the rap game's most prolific artists, and he was as close with Bulletface as Meek Mill was with Rick Ross.

People had begun to recognize Tamera and Tirzah from the viral social media photos Bulletface and Alexus had posted on their Instagram pages last Friday. Someone commented that with T-Walk, Young Meach, and the girls from the pictures (Tirzah and Tamera) all here in the same club, it was only a matter of time before Bulletface and Alexus walked in. Rell looked over at Tamera and smiled. He could only imagine how uncomfortable he would feel being around the power couple after he had fucked Alexus just five days ago.

Lil Phil was too busy on his iPhone to notice all the attention Tamera and Tirzah were being given. He was on the opposite side of the table from Tamera and Rell, drinking from a large bottle of Remy that Rell had watched him drop a handful of pills into. Rell and Tamera were sharing a bottle of Moet, taking tiny sips every ten minutes or so. Krystal was standing next to Rell's chair, vibing to the music. Young M.A.'s "Eat" was the jam of the moment.

Rell took Krystal's elbow and pulled her close. "I heard you're getting kicked out of your apartment," he said, trying not to scream it too loud.

"Yeah," Krystal said. "I'll be good, though. I found a place out by Lakeland Projects. It's a four-bedroom with a full basement. I'll be able to get it. My grandma's giving me the loan to pay the security deposit. I'll have her paid back in seven or eight months."

"How much will it cost to get moved all the way in?"

"About fifteen hundred. I'm getting my cable and Internet transferred there on the first of the year, and we'll be moving in on the third. Granny's sending me eight hundred to help out."

Shaking his head, Rell pulled out his big wad of cash and began peeling through hundreds. He had come to Michigan City with a little over ten thousand dollars in his pocket. Realizing what he was doing, Tamera kissed him hard on the cheek.

"You don't have to do this," Krystal said.

"You ain't gotta tell me that." Rell kept thumbing through the hundred-dollar bills. "My father always told me that God gives us blessings not only to enjoy for ourselves but also to pass on to others. You seem like a good enough person to me."

He handed Krystal $4,500 in bank-new hundreds, and his wife treated him to another passionate cheek-peck. Krystal's soft lips tapped against his other cheek. He was saved from the torture of watching the tears fall down Krystal's pretty face. Lil Phil stood up at that very moment and motioned for Rell to follow him.

"Pops just pulled up," Lil Phil said.

It was Rell's turn to peck Tamera on the cheek. At least that's what he intended to do. She turned at the last second and pressed her lips to his, holding his face in her hands, peering into his eyes with a look that said *you'd better be careful*.

He trailed Lil Phil away from their table, flicking his eyes in every direction. The club was crammed full of people. Rell loved seeing black women in revealing attire, and there was no shortage of them on the spacious hardwood floor inside of Club Manna's. Women of every size and shape - slim-thick, BBWs, and everything between the two - danced and drank and smiled and laughed all around Rell as he and Lil Phil forged a path toward the front door.

They were halfway across the floor when elated screams began to emanate from the rear of the club. Huge, shrieking screams.

"It's Alexus and Bulletface!" some girl yelled at the very top of her lungs.

The crowd went rushing toward the VIP section even more urgently than they had when T-Walk first emerged from the fogged glass door. Rell looked back to see if it was indeed the most wealthy and powerful married couple in black America and found that it was. Even from here in the middle of the floor. he could see them quite clearly. Both of them were wearing all white, and they had about a dozen black-suited bodyguards surrounding them.

Lil Phil looked from the VIP section to Rell and then back to the VIP section again. He seemed almost as excited as the women. "Bro, that's Bulletface?" His eyebrows lifted, and his forehead became a maze of keep wrinkles.

"Let's get out here to your pops," Rell said.

"Go ahead. He'll be in a red minivan with Bugs Bunny hanging from the rearview mirror." Lil Phil left no room for protest. He went waddling off in the direction of the crowd.

Rell pulled on the hood of his black Moncler sweatshirt and soldiered on through the club, grimly determined to avenge his brother's attempted murder. He strolled bravely out the door and then stopped, swiveling his head from left to right. *Red minivan, red minivan, red minivan.* He didn't see any red minivans. There were two white minivans, and a brown one. There was a green Dodge minivan parked two spaces to the right of his Benz. But he didn't see a red...

"There you go," Rell murmured, and took off in a jog toward his Mercedes. There was a red minivan, but it was exiting the parking lot.

Why in the fuck was it leaving?

The minivan crossed Michigan Boulevard and pulled into a gas station directly across from Club Manna's just as Rell was settling behind the steering wheel of the Benz. He started the engine and scooped the Glock up from under his seat. "It's yo' aaaaass, Mr. Postman," he said, quoting the movie *Friday* for some odd reason as he eased out of his parking spot and made a beeline for the exit, keeping an unwavering eye on the minivan. He wanted a cigarette - *needed* a cigarette - but this was no time for a smoke.

The passenger seat area was a throbbing force field of sour stink. It was so horrendously putrid that Rell had to lower all the windows to keep from being overpowered by the stench. *That fat motherfucker farted in my car before he got out*, Rell thought to himself, shaking his head with a grimace of disgust.

He made it to the parking lot exit and braked for a long moment. He watched two men get out of the minivan and head into the gas station. One of them looked rail-thin and was wearing a jacket that was as gray as the braided cornrows on his head. The other man wore an orange-colored hoodie with the hood pulled halfway onto his head, as if his only mission in life was to keep his ears warm; damn the rest of his head.

Rell had watched *The First 48* enough to know that a gas station was not a good place to murder someone. Those cameras were a bitch. He'd done time with a guy who had been sentenced to life for committing a double homicide that was captured on video surveillance at a gas station on the south side of Chicago.

He noticed there was an alleyway that ran alongside the gas station. He crossed Michigan Boulevard and entered the rocky alleyway in a haste. He stopped next to the station's red brick wall, threw the transmission into park, and got out with his fingers closed tightly around the butt of his Glock.

The alleyway was dark. Rell walked slowly to the front corner of the building, like an old man afflicted with a terrible base of arthritis, hearing and feeling the small rocks shifting under his feet. He clenched his teeth and took an enormous breath. An image of his little brother lying in a bloody heap flashed in his mind and strengthened his resolve.

The wind gusted. Snow rattled against the side of the sparkling white Benz. He dipped his head forward and peered around the corner of the building. The two men were just stepping out of the gas station, but it was what Rell saw beyond the pumps that grabbed his attention.

There were more than a dozen police vehicles lined up in front of a large building about a block away from Club Manna's. It took

142

him only a second to conclude that he was looking at a police station.

Rell didn't give himself time to think it over. He stepped out from beside the building, holding the pistol in both hands. He realized coolly that he would be shooting a man dead while the most rich and famous woman on the planet posed for photos in the VIP room of the nightclub across the street.

The man with the graying cornrows was the man who'd shot Jah. He glanced at Rell, and Rell fired twice, striking him in the chest. Then Rell turned and shot the man in the orange hoodie twice in the back as he attempted to flee, and he went down like his friend. Rell drew a bead on old Gray Braids and squeezed the trigger two more times. The bullets cut perfect holes in the skin under the man's left eye just as he was looking up at Rell.

Two seconds later, Rell was back in the Mercedes, dropping the trans into drive and slamming down on the gas pedal. His tires churned up rocks as the car rocketed forward. At the end of the alleyway, he made a hard right turn onto a street, then an equally hard left at the next corner. He sped down four whole blocks, completely disregarding the stop signs. Finally, he pushed the hood of his sweater back and slowed the car down from sixty miles an hour to twenty. He veered into another alleyway, wrapped the Glock in his hoodie, and stuffed it down into someone's trash can.

"Shit," he said, reversing out of the alley just as the sound of police sirens began to wail in the distance.

He took out Tamera's cell phone and composed a text message with one nervously trembling thumb.

King Rio

Chapter 21

Get Tirz and hit the highway right now!
Tamera read the message twice. Her heart dived down in her chest without a bungee cord or a parachute. She put on the world's fakest smile and looked up at the world's richest woman.

Alexus had just walked over to Tamera's table. She was flanked by five broad-shouldered bodyguards that looked like Secret Service agents. The white fur coat Alexus had on was bright as the huge white diamonds on her neck, wrists, and perfectly manicured fingers. She bent over and put her mouth an inch away from Tamera's right ear.

"Have you told someone about what happened between us last week? Shake your head yes or no."

Tamera shook her head from left to right. Beyond Alexus's bodyguards, she could see Bulletface and Young Meach wading through the crowd on the main floor, taking pictures with screaming fans. Everyone seemed twice as excited to see Bulletface as they had been to see T-Walk. Many of the girls were crying real tears.

"Well," Alexus said, "*some*body told him. I'm sure he didn't just pull it out of thin air. And what are you and Tirzah doing here with T-Walk? What did he do, find you two to ask about me and Blake?"

Tamera swiveled her head, left-right-left. "We came here for somebody else," she said, getting up. "I have to go."

"No. I want you to come with me. You need to convince my husband that nothing happened between us."

"We're in my sister's car," Tamera explained, "and those two girls over there came with us. We have to take them home first."

"My men - I'll have one of them drive your car. They'll take your girls home and then bring your car to us in Chicago. Deal?" Alexus extended a hand for Tamera to shake.

Tamera looked at the hand, thought about it, and then shook the hand, sealing the deal. She didn't feel like driving. She felt like relaxing, maybe having a blunt and a stiff drink to help her ease into that elusive realm of relaxation.

A wave of important whispers had begun to spread throughout the club. There had been a shooting at "The Duke" and somebody was dead. Lil Phil was just climbing the VIP steps when a dark-skinned man with gold teeth gave him three hard taps on the shoulder and some words in the ear, and all of a sudden, Lil Phil turned around and went plowing through the crowd.

Tamera pulled Tirzah aside and quickly explained the situation. Tirzah gave the car keys to one of Alexus's men while Tamera told Krystal and Keyanna what was going on. A moment later, Tamera and Tirzah were following Alexus through a hallway beyond the VIP door. They emerged into an alleyway guarded by uniformed policemen. There were three white Mercedes Sprinter vans and four white Cadillac Escalades parked side to side off to the left of the door, and to the right three blue exotic cars were parked.

"Looks like some kind of presidential motorcade," Tirzah commented.

They were being led toward the open sliding door of one of the Mercedes vans.

"It does," Tamera murmured, but she sounded absent, not really listening. Her mind was racing. Rell had succeeded in catching the guy who'd tried to kill Jah, but would he get away with it? Also, Alexus was without a doubt the most famous woman in America (quite possibly the most attractive one, as well), and it did feel good being in the same space as a person of such fame, but what about those stories of all the people who had lost their lives for being around Alexus? Was it safe being around Alexus? She didn't believe it was.

Every inch of the Sprinte's interior was spotless. There were six white leather seats, two facing the other four. The windows were hidden behind white shutters. The walls were white with burled walnut panels, and that same glossy wood framed the glass doors of a lighted cabinet that displayed three bottles of Hennessy.

Tamera and Tirzah went to the rearmost two seats on the side of the four and sat down. Tamera immediately dialed her own cell phone number on Rell's iPhone.

"You leave yet?" Rell said as soon as he picked up.

"We're leaving now."

"Don't leave with that fat nigga."

"No, no - he ran off. Some guy told him something just as he was about to come back to our table, and he turned around and ran off toward the front door."

"Hurry up and get out of there before he comes back."

"We're out of the club," Tamera said, glancing up at Alexus as the queen of everything sat down in one of the two seats that faced the four. "You're not going to believe this, but we're actually in this big luxury Mercedes van with Alexus Costilla. Her and Bulletface showed up right after you left."

"I know. I saw 'em. Why are you with them?"

"One of her bodyguards is driving the car. It's safer that way. You know I was drinking, and now Tirz is drunk off her ass." She lowered her voice to a whisper. "And somebody told Bulletface about...you know...the concert. She wants me to convince him that nothing happened."

Rell paused. Across the aisle, Tirzah was on FaceTime with Bubbles, who had apparently gotten engaged to Juice a few hours ago. She was showing Tirzah the ring and telling her about a cele-bration that was going to kick off at Redbone's Gentleman's Club in forty-five minutes or so.

"Just hurry up and leave," Rell said finally. "I'm about to hit the highway now. I'll call you back in fifteen minutes."

"Okay. I love you."

"Love you too."

"Don't be driving like a maniac," Tamera added worriedly. "Obey the speed limit. And put on your seat belt. You can't afford to get pulled over at a time like this."

Rell chuckled. "This ain't my first rodeo. I know what I'm do-ing. Let me get off this phone before I fuck around and get pulled over."

"Okay." Tamera sighed. "Call me back in exactly fifteen minutes. I'm counting."

Rell was chuckling again as he ended the call.

A black smog of worry had descended upon Tamera. She lifted her head and saw that Alexus was watching her. Those keen, calculating green eyes were locked on Tamera's honey brown ones. Alexus had her legs crossed, and she had an iPhone in her hand. A questionable smile played at the edges of her mouth.

"I see here on Instagram that Bubbles really is engaged," Alexus said, glancing down at her phone and then returning her gaze to Tamera. "She looks amazing in that dress."

"I'm on FaceTime with her now!" Tirzah bellowed, as if her loud-ass voice had not revealed that fact several moments ago.

Calmly, Alexus turned to Tirzah and asked her to hang up the phone, Tirzah complied with a tight Face, but not before telling Bubbles that she would see her at Redbone's. Alexus smiled rather faintly; and, in somewhat of a hesitating manner, she seemed to give consent.

Tamera was deeply stirred. A tear stole down her cheek. A vision of Rell handcuffed in the back seat of a police car floated before her. What would she do if Rell got himself arrested for murder? Die, she decided. She would die like Debbie Reynolds died the day after her beloved daughter Carrie Fisher died. Her heart wouldn't be strong enough to suffer the loss of a man as loving and caring as Sincere Jerrell Owens.

"Blake's on the way out now," Alexus said, glancing again at her iPhone. "Remember this: I was at the restaurant with all of you this past Friday. When we got to the Staples Center, we went *straight* to Blake's dressing room, and then he brought me out on stage with him. We never went to that other dressing room. Comprende?"

Tamera and Tirzah nodded their heads in unison.

Seconds later, the side door slid open. Tamera's breath caught in her throat when Bulletface stepped in - she was starstruck, she realized - but the shock of her life came when she watched T-Walk and Thunder step in after him. T-Walk, who was Bulletface's longtime nemesis. It was like watching Drake and Meek Mill get in a van together, only it was more shocking because Bulletface and T-Walk's beef had taken place the *real* way, in the streets. No Twitter fingers, all trigger fingers. Bodies had accumulated on both sides of the war - Tenth Street Hustlers and Dub Life Goons; Vice Lords and Gangster Disciples.

Bulletface took the seat next to his wife, and T-Walk sat across from him. Thunder took the seat across from Alexus, the one right in front of Tamera. The door slid shut, and the Sprinter drove off between the other two Sprinters.

"I can't believe this," Tamera said. "Bulletface and T-Walk sitting right across from each other. I wish I could take a picture of this. This is a picture everybody needs to see, not the pictures social media keeps using to tear you all apart."

"Fuck a picture," Bulletface said, reaching out and shaking T-Walk's hand. "Last time we was in this alley together, we almost killed each other. We're from the same city. They want us to be at each other's throats. I can't let it go like they want it to go. I'd rather end this shit like Hove and Nas than to end it like Pac and Biggie."

"For real, though," T-Walk said, nodding in agreement. "I'm done with all that beef shit anyway. The only nigga I wanna get at is whoever killed my brothers in Chicago last year."

"I lost my sister that same day in Chicago," Alexus said. "She shot Lil Cholly and Cup, and their guys shot her. It all went down on Chicago Avenue, at The Visionary Lounge. Your brothers were killed on the same street. The Visionary Lounge reopened about three months ago. Cup's son - Bankroll Reese - owns it now. Blake and I went to the grand opening. We weren't in there a good five minutes before somebody got killed in the parking lot."

"You think Bankroll Reese might know something about my brothers getting killed that day?" T-Walk asked.

Alexus shrugged. "Only one way to find out," she said. "We're about to go to his strip club now. Ask him yourself."

King Rio

150

Chapter 22

By 11:30 p.m. the crowded party scene was warmed all the way up. With the rap-music background, the stages inside of Redbone's Gentleman's Club looked like a great big sexy rap video where the strippers were the stars. The floor was covered in one-dollar bills - thousands upon thousands of them - and thousands more were being thrown in the air every couple of seconds.

Juice had tossed $20,000. Bubbles had thrown another twenty grand at her own cousin. Bankroll Reese and Shawnna had showered the curvy strippers with about fifty thousand dollars. Their table was to the right of Juice's, and the next table was where the real money was. Bulletface and Alexus had just arrived. They were throwing hundred-dollar bills in the air, big stacks of them, and they had the baddest strippers in the club tonight - a yellow bone with red hair and a lot of colorful tattoos on her body - at their table. T-Walk and his reality TV star girlfriend were at the table with them. Half of the smartphones in the club were taking pictures and videos of Bulletface and Alexus. Rell, Tamera, and Tirzah were sharing the table with Juice and Bubbles.

Juice sat down, and the stripper in front of him began to give him a lap dance. Her name was Candy. She was quite talented with her dancing skills, but he wasn't paying much attention to her.

His mind was stuck on the two homicide detectives in the black Dodge Challenger.

He had seen them sitting in the Challenger in front of the strip club when he pulled up. There were two CPD patrol cars out there too. He had no idea what they were doing, but he had a bad feeling about it. A terrible, gut-twisting feeling.

"Baby," Juice said, taking his new finance's elbow, "Come 'ere." He pulled her close, inhaled through his nostrils the alluring scent of her Chanel perfume, and smiled a tiny smile.

"Can you believe Blake and Alexus actually came to our engagement turn up?" Bubbles said, beaming.

"Can you believe we just saw those two cops again?" Juice thought this was the more important question. "They're investigating somebody in here. It's either me or somebody close to me."

"You're being paranoid."

"I'm being smart," Juice said decisively. "But it's okay. We'll be good either way it goes. I'm out of the game now. I just hope I didn't wait until it was too late."

Bubbles shook her head and planted a kiss on his lips. He put his hands on the big round swells of her ass and squeezed.

"It wasn't too late," she said. "Don't even think that way."

Juice didn't want to think that way, but he couldn't help it. He'd been a street nigga all his life. He had a hustler's intuition, and right now it was telling him that those cops were posted up outside for a reason. Either they were watching the people going in or they were waiting for somebody to come out. Maybe they didn't have enough evidence to get a warrant to come inside the club, so they were waiting for their suspect to come to them. But who might the two homicide detectives be waiting on to exit the strip club?

"Tamia!" Juice bellowed suddenly. He took a step toward Tamia as she swung around and grabbed her hips.

"What?" Tamia said.

"Chandra and Marshall got killed right outside your apartment."

"And?"

"What did you tell the police?"

"Did Chandra call or text you before she came over there?"

Tamia nodded. Standing there in her red-lace thong, braless and drizzled in glitter, she bore a striking resemblance to Bubbles. Her creamy brown complexion was flawless. Her breasts were perfect globes of soft flesh. "She called me right before she pulled up."

"One of the first things cops do," Juice said, "is check the victim's phone to see who was the last person they talked to. If you told them that you didn't know the victim, and they found your number in her phone with your name right over it, what do you think is going to happen?"

He saw the fear register in her eyes. She raised her eyebrows, flicked her eyes from Juice to Bubbles and back to Juice again, and then muttered, "Aw shit."

"Dumbass," Bubbles said snappishly. "You're the damn reason those cops are out there. They're here for your dumb ass."

The fear in Tamia's sweet brown eyes spread to her face, and she crossed her arms over her naked tits, shifting her weight from one leg to the other. Bankroll Reese came over to see what was going on, while Candy went and joined the red-haired stripper who was dancing for Bulletface.

"Do you think I'm about to get arrested?" Tamia asked.

"Arrested?" Reese said. "Arrested for what?"

"For lying to those police officers when they asked if I knew Chandra and Marshall. She had just called me before she pulled up. We talked this morning and last night too. Shit. I wasn't thinking. I wasn't thinking at all. I just wanted to get out of there."

Bankroll Reese told her to pick up her money and head to the locker room. Two bouncers with push-brooms helped sweep all the dollars into one large pile and stuff it all into a black plastic trash bag.

"This shit just gets crazier and crazier," Reese said to Juice. "That nigga T-Walk asked me if I knew anything about his brothers getting killed the night my pops got killed. How in the fuck am I supposed to know that? And Kev just told me that it was T-Walk who sent the shooters on Trumbull that night I got shot a few years back. Plus, Alexus's sister was the bitch who shot my pops. I should have the gang push on all of 'em."

The "gang" Bankroll Reese was referring to was Cup Gang, a Money-flashing, jewelry-wearing, gun-toting, gangbanging conglomerate of Four Corner Hustlers and Traveling Vice Lords. About thirty of them were in the building. They were young guys who had for the most part attended high school with Reese. There were several other West Side cliques in the building, the largest of which was Sicko Mobb. Like Cup Gang, Sicko Mobb was made up entirely of North Lawndale gang members.

All the cognac Juice had ingested today was taking a toll on his brain. His head felt as if it was swinging left and right. He glanced to his right and saw that Bulletface and Alexus were in an up-close conversation with Tamera and Rell. T-Walk and his girlfriend were talking with the squad of Gangster Disciples that had come with drill rapper King Louie.

"Nah," Juice said to Reese. "Let 'em slide. Give 'em a clean slate. From what I have, Alexus wasn't that close with her sister anyway, and T-Walk is a businessman. I'm getting money with Bulletface. Let's not lose focus, you feel me? If it don't make dollars, it don't make sense."

Bankroll Reese was nodding his head in agreement and getting ready to say something when Juice spoke again.

"I got whole slabs for the fifteen. Not for everybody; I'd be a dummy to play it like that with everybody. Just you, Wayno, Kev, Rell, Jah. The big dogs, you know? The New Year is on the way in a few days. Let's turn 2017 upside down. Let's fuck the game up and loot the city."

Reese nodded again, adjusted the big diamond ring on his pinkie finger, and looked at Tamia as she came sauntering back from the locker room, dressed in jeans and a coat.

"I'm about to sneak out the back door," Tamia said.

Juice shook his head. "Nah. Just, uhh…go on out there. If they take you in for questioning, don't say shit - especially about those pick-ups and drop offs. Ask for a lawyer right away. If they arrest you, I'll have you bonded right out. Just make sure you keep your fucking mouth shut. As long as you do that, everything'll work out fine."

"We'll go out there with you," Bubbles said, and hugged her younger relative. "You'll be good. Don't even worry about that shit."

They all headed toward the door - Juice, Bubbles, Tamia; Reese, his two main bodyguards, and the twins, a couple of Cup Gang members. Juice was ready to leave anyway. He'd had enough food and drinks for the day. Now what he needed was some sleep. And maybe a little sex.

His assumption was correct: Tamia walked out the door and was promptly taken into custody. Dawn muttered something under her breath as Tamia was being handcuffed, and Shawnna laughed. Juice stuffed Tamia's bag full of cash into the trunk of his rented Mercedes Maybach and then got in the back seat with Bubbles. She phoned her sister, Kisha, who came out of the club and got in the driver's seat just as the cops were racing off with Tamia. Kisha pulled off a moment later.

"Blake and T-Walk were actually hanging out together," Bubbles said with a hint of incredulity in her voice. "I don't know how that's even possible. Everybody knows that Blake and T-Walk have been at each other's throats for years. I can't lie, though - it's good to see two black men settle their differences without one of them getting killed." she paused, gazed longingly at her ring, and then added, "not that it matters to me one way or the other. I'm just happy for us, happy for our situation."

Juice snaked an arm around her lower back. Pulling her close, he gave Lakita Thomas a kiss on the cheek and inflated his lungs with a deep nasal inhalation of her perfume. He ruminated about the engagement and concluded that he too was happy for himself and Bubbles. He was a drug kingpin with the baddest bitch in the city by his side. On top of the world is where he was, and he intended to stay there.

King Rio

Epilogue

The interrogation room's fluorescent fixtures sent down relentless lights. The room was refrigerator-cold. There were two cameras on the ceiling, one in the left corner behind Tamia, the other in the right corner in front of her, right above the door.

Tamia had emptied the bottle of water the police officer gave her when she was led into the room, and now she was in need of a restroom break to relieve her distended bladder.

Jesus Christ, she thought, *how long have I been in this damn room?*

Two hours, at the very least. Quite possibly five. Shit, it seemed like a whole twenty-four had passed. Tamia was ready to get it all over with. She was ready to ask for a lawyer, get booked into Cook County Jail, and then bond out and go home.

When the door finally swung inward, Tamia blurted out, "I need to use the bathroom. Like, ASAP."

The two brawny white men were identified by the names stitched on their shirts: Homicide Detective J.W. Bryant and R. Milam. Neither detective spoke. Milam shut the door. They stood at the other side of the table and looked down at Tamia. Their expressions were grim.

"I'm not answering any questions without having a lawyer present," Tamia said indignantly. "And I really need to use the bathroom."

Milam chuckled once and crossed his huge arms over his muscular chest. Bryant put the palms of his veiny white hands on the table and leaned forward until his face was mere inches away from Tamia's, so close that she could smell the stink of cigarette on his breath.

"Listen up," Bryant said aggressively, "and listen close, because I'm only going to say this once. You're in a shitload of trouble. A real fucking shitload."

Milam produced a roll of photos from his pants pocket and spread them out on the table. There were photographs of Juice and Bubbles sitting in her Benz, photos of Juice's apartment building on

Drake Avenue, and, most damaging of all, images from the video surveillance cameras outside of Tamia's apartment that captured Lil Mark and his friend coming and going and then Chandra and Marshall coming and going. There were also captured images of Chandra's final moments of existence, her sprinting back to Tamia's door and getting it slammed in her face, her pounding on the door with two closed fists until a bullet passed through her back.

The photos brought tears to Tamia's eyes.

"Now," Bryant said slowly and deliberately, "if you want a lawyer present, we'll walk out now, book you for two counts of accessory to murder, felony drug possession - yeah, we found the X pills in your purse - obstruction, interfering with a homicide investigation, and whatever other charges we can pin on you, and you can think about all of this in jail, because you won't have a bond."

No bond? Tamia wriggled her butt from side to side on the padded folding chair, struggling not only to keep her bladder in check but also to understand the full ramifications of the charges she was facing.

"Or," Bryant continued, "you can tell us who the shooters were and who this guy" - he jabbed a forefinger at the photo of Juice and Bubbles - "is and go home with no charges. It's all on you."

Tamia began to cry, and then, a moment later, she began to talk.

THE END

Lock Down Publications and Ca$h Presents assisted publishing packages.

BASIC PACKAGE $499
Editing
Cover Design
Formatting

UPGRADED PACKAGE $800
Typing
Editing
Cover Design
Formatting

ADVANCE PACKAGE $1,200
Typing
Editing
Cover Design
Formatting
Copyright registration
Proofreading
Upload book to Amazon

LDP SUPREME PACKAGE $1,500
Typing
Editing
Cover Design
Formatting
Copyright registration
Proofreading
Set up Amazon account
Upload book to Amazon
Advertise on LDP Amazon and Facebook page

***Other services available upon request. Additional charges may apply
**Lock Down Publications
P.O. Box 944
Stockbridge, GA 30281-9998
Phone # 470 303-9761**

Submission Guideline

Submit the first three chapters of your completed manuscript to ldpsubmissions@gmail.com, subject line: Your book's title. The manuscript must be in a .doc file and sent as an attachment. Document should be in Times New Roman, double spaced and in size 12 font. Also, provide your synopsis and full contact information. If sending multiple submissions, they must each be in a separate email.

Have a story but no way to send it electronically? You can still submit to LDP/Ca$h Presents. Send in the first three chapters, written or typed, of your completed manuscript to:

LDP: Submissions Dept
Po Box 944
Stockbridge, Ga 30281

DO NOT send original manuscript. Must be a duplicate.

Provide your synopsis and a cover letter containing your full contact information.

Thanks for considering LDP and Ca$h Presents.

<u>NEW RELEASES</u>

LOYALTY IS EVERYTHING by MOLOTTI
HERE TODAY GONE TOMORROW by FLY ROCK
A GANGSTA'S KARMA 3 by FLAME
BORN IN THE GRAVE 2 by SELF MADE TAY
THE BRICK MAN 5 by KING RIO

King Rio

STRAIGHT BEAST MODE III

De'Kari

KINGPIN KILLAZ IV

STREET KINGS III

PAID IN BLOOD III

CARTEL KILLAZ IV

DOPE GODS III

Hood Rich

SINS OF A HUSTLA II

ASAD

YAYO V

Bred In The Game 2

S. Allen

THE STREETS WILL TALK II

By Yolanda Moore

SON OF A DOPE FIEND III

HEAVEN GOT A GHETTO II

SKI MASK MONEY II

By Renta

LOYALTY AIN'T PROMISED III

By Keith Williams

I'M NOTHING WITHOUT HIS LOVE II

SINS OF A THUG II

TO THE THUG I LOVED BEFORE II

IN A HUSTLER I TRUST II

By Monet Dragun

QUIET MONEY IV

EXTENDED CLIP III

THUG LIFE IV

By **Trai'Quan**

The Brick Man 5

THE STREETS MADE ME IV

By **Larry D. Wright**

IF YOU CROSS ME ONCE II

ANGEL V

By **Anthony Fields**

THE STREETS WILL NEVER CLOSE IV

By **K'ajji**

HARD AND RUTHLESS III

KILLA KOUNTY IV

By **Khufu**

MONEY GAME III

By **Smoove Dolla**

JACK BOYS VS DOPE BOYS IV

A GANGSTA'S QUR'AN V

COKE GIRLZ II

COKE BOYS II

LIFE OF A SAVAGE V

CHI'RAQ GANGSTAS V

By **Romell Tukes**

MURDA WAS THE CASE III

Elijah R. Freeman

THE STREETS NEVER LET GO III

By **Robert Baptiste**

AN UNFORESEEN LOVE IV

BABY, I'M WINTERTIME COLD II

By **Meesha**

MONEY MAFIA II

By **Jibril Williams**

QUEEN OF THE ZOO III

165

King Rio

By **Black Migo**
VICIOUS LOYALTY III
By **Kingpen**
A GANGSTA'S PAIN III
By **J-Blunt**
CONFESSIONS OF A JACKBOY III
By **Nicholas Lock**
GRIMEY WAYS III
By **Ray Vinci**
KING KILLA II
By **Vincent "Vitto" Holloway**
BETRAYAL OF A THUG III
By **Fre$h**
THE MURDER QUEENS III
By **Michael Gallon**
THE BIRTH OF A GANGSTER III
By **Delmont Player**
TREAL LOVE II
By **Le'Monica Jackson**
FOR THE LOVE OF BLOOD III
By **Jamel Mitchell**
RAN OFF ON DA PLUG II
By **Paper Boi Rari**
HOOD CONSIGLIERE III
By **Keese**
PRETTY GIRLS DO NASTY THINGS II
By **Nicole Goosby**
PROTÉGÉ OF A LEGEND II
By **Corey Robinson**
IT'S JUST ME AND YOU II

The Brick Man 5

By Ah'Million
BORN IN THE GRAVE III
By Self Made Tay
FOREVER GANGSTA III
By Adrian Dulan
GORILLAZ IN THE TRENCHES II
By SayNoMore
THE COCAINE PRINCESS VI
By King Rio
CRIME BOSS II
Playa Ray
LOYALTY IS EVERYTHING II
Molotti
HERE TODAY GONE TOMORROW II
By Fly Rock

Available Now

RESTRAINING ORDER I & II
By CA$H & Coffee
LOVE KNOWS NO BOUNDARIES I II & III
By Coffee
RAISED AS A GOON I, II, III & IV
BRED BY THE SLUMS I, II, III
BLAST FOR ME I & II
ROTTEN TO THE CORE I II III
A BRONX TALE I, II, III

King Rio

DUFFLE BAG CARTEL I II III IV V VI

HEARTLESS GOON I II III IV V

A SAVAGE DOPEBOY I II

DRUG LORDS I II III

CUTTHROAT MAFIA I II

KING OF THE TRENCHES

By **Ghost**

LAY IT DOWN **I & II**

LAST OF A DYING BREED I II

BLOOD STAINS OF A SHOTTA I & II III

By **Jamaica**

LOYAL TO THE GAME I II III

LIFE OF SIN I, II III

By **TJ & Jelissa**

BLOODY COMMAS I & II

SKI MASK CARTEL I II & III

KING OF NEW YORK I II,III IV V

RISE TO POWER I II III

COKE KINGS I II III IV V

BORN HEARTLESS I II III IV

KING OF THE TRAP I II

By **T.J. Edwards**

IF LOVING HIM IS WRONG…I & II

LOVE ME EVEN WHEN IT HURTS I II III

By **Jelissa**

WHEN THE STREETS CLAP BACK I & II III

THE HEART OF A SAVAGE I II III IV

MONEY MAFIA

LOYAL TO THE SOIL I II III

By **Jibril Williams**

The Brick Man 5

A DISTINGUISHED THUG STOLE MY HEART I II & III

LOVE SHOULDN'T HURT I II III IV

RENEGADE BOYS I II III IV

PAID IN KARMA I II III

SAVAGE STORMS I II III

AN UNFORESEEN LOVE I II III

BABY, I'M WINTERTIME COLD

By **Meesha**

A GANGSTER'S CODE I &, II III

A GANGSTER'S SYN I II III

THE SAVAGE LIFE I II III

CHAINED TO THE STREETS I II III

BLOOD ON THE MONEY I II III

A GANGSTA'S PAIN I II

By J-Blunt

PUSH IT TO THE LIMIT

By **Bre' Hayes**

BLOOD OF A BOSS **I, II, III, IV, V**

SHADOWS OF THE GAME

TRAP BASTARD

By **Askari**

THE STREETS BLEED MURDER **I, II & III**

THE HEART OF A GANGSTA I II& III

By **Jerry Jackson**

CUM FOR ME I II III IV V VI VII VIII

An **LDP Erotica Collaboration**

BRIDE OF A HUSTLA **I II & II**

THE FETTI GIRLS **I, II& III**

CORRUPTED BY A GANGSTA I, II III, IV

BLINDED BY HIS LOVE

King Rio

THE PRICE YOU PAY FOR LOVE I, II ,III

DOPE GIRL MAGIC I II III

By **Destiny Skai**

WHEN A GOOD GIRL GOES BAD

By **Adrienne**

THE COST OF LOYALTY I II III

By Kweli

A GANGSTER'S REVENGE **I II III & IV**

THE BOSS MAN'S DAUGHTERS I II III IV V

A SAVAGE LOVE **I & II**

BAE BELONGS TO ME I II

A HUSTLER'S DECEIT I, II, III

WHAT BAD BITCHES DO I, II, III

SOUL OF A MONSTER I II III

KILL ZONE

A DOPE BOY'S QUEEN I II III

TIL DEATH

By **Aryanna**

A KINGPIN'S AMBITON

A KINGPIN'S AMBITION **II**

I MURDER FOR THE DOUGH

By **Ambitious**

TRUE SAVAGE I II III IV V VI VII

DOPE BOY MAGIC I, II, III

MIDNIGHT CARTEL I II III

CITY OF KINGZ I II

NIGHTMARE ON SILENT AVE

THE PLUG OF LIL MEXICO II

CLASSIC CITY

By **Chris Green**

A DOPEBOY'S PRAYER

By **Eddie "Wolf" Lee**

THE KING CARTEL **I, II & III**

By **Frank Gresham**

THESE NIGGAS AIN'T LOYAL **I, II & III**

By **Nikki Tee**

GANGSTA SHYT **I II &III**

By **CATO**

THE ULTIMATE BETRAYAL

By **Phoenix**

BOSS'N UP **I , II & III**

By **Royal Nicole**

I LOVE YOU TO DEATH

By **Destiny J**

I RIDE FOR MY HITTA

I STILL RIDE FOR MY HITTA

By **Misty Holt**

LOVE & CHASIN' PAPER

By **Qay Crockett**

TO DIE IN VAIN

SINS OF A HUSTLA

By **ASAD**

BROOKLYN HUSTLAZ

By **Boogsy Morina**

BROOKLYN ON LOCK I & II

By **Sonovia**

GANGSTA CITY

By **Teddy Duke**

A DRUG KING AND HIS DIAMOND I & II III

A DOPEMAN'S RICHES

King Rio

HER MAN, MINE'S TOO I, II

CASH MONEY HO'S

THE WIFEY I USED TO BE I II

PRETTY GIRLS DO NASTY THINGS

By Nicole Goosby

TRAPHOUSE KING **I II & III**

KINGPIN KILLAZ I II III

STREET KINGS I II

PAID IN BLOOD **I II**

CARTEL KILLAZ I II III

DOPE GODS I II

By **Hood Rich**

LIPSTICK KILLAH **I, II, III**

CRIME OF PASSION I II & III

FRIEND OR FOE I II III

By **Mimi**

STEADY MOBBN' **I, II, III**

THE STREETS STAINED MY SOUL I II III

By **Marcellus Allen**

WHO SHOT YA **I, II, III**

SON OF A DOPE FIEND I II

HEAVEN GOT A GHETTO

SKI MASK MONEY

Renta

GORILLAZ IN THE BAY **I II III IV**

TEARS OF A GANGSTA I II

3X KRAZY I II

STRAIGHT BEAST MODE I II

DE'KARI

TRIGGADALE I II III

The Brick Man 5

MURDAROBER WAS THE CASE I II
Elijah R. Freeman
GOD BLESS THE TRAPPERS I, II, III
THESE SCANDALOUS STREETS I, II, III
FEAR MY GANGSTA I, II, III IV, V
THESE STREETS DON'T LOVE NOBODY I, II
BURY ME A G I, II, III, IV, V
A GANGSTA'S EMPIRE I, II, III, IV
THE DOPEMAN'S BODYGAURD I II
THE REALEST KILLAZ I II III
THE LAST OF THE OGS I II III
Tranay Adams
THE STREETS ARE CALLING
Duquie Wilson
MARRIED TO A BOSS I II III
By Destiny Skai & Chris Green
KINGZ OF THE GAME I II III IV V VI
CRIME BOSS
Playa Ray
SLAUGHTER GANG I II III
RUTHLESS HEART I II III
By Willie Slaughter
FUK SHYT
By Blakk Diamond
DON'T F#CK WITH MY HEART I II
By Linnea
ADDICTED TO THE DRAMA I II III
IN THE ARM OF HIS BOSS II
By Jamila
YAYO I II III IV

A SHOOTER'S AMBITION I II

BRED IN THE GAME

By S. Allen

TRAP GOD I II III

RICH $AVAGE I II III

MONEY IN THE GRAVE I II III

By Martell Troublesome Bolden

FOREVER GANGSTA I II

GLOCKS ON SATIN SHEETS I II

By Adrian Dulan

TOE TAGZ I II III IV

LEVELS TO THIS SHYT I II

IT'S JUST ME AND YOU

By Ah'Million

KINGPIN DREAMS I II III

RAN OFF ON DA PLUG

By Paper Boi Rari

CONFESSIONS OF A GANGSTA I II III IV

CONFESSIONS OF A JACKBOY I II

By Nicholas Lock

I'M NOTHING WITHOUT HIS LOVE

SINS OF A THUG

TO THE THUG I LOVED BEFORE

A GANGSTA SAVED XMAS

IN A HUSTLER I TRUST

By Monet Dragun

CAUGHT UP IN THE LIFE I II III

THE STREETS NEVER LET GO I II

By Robert Baptiste

NEW TO THE GAME I II III

The Brick Man 5

MONEY, MURDER & MEMORIES I II III

By **Malik D. Rice**

LIFE OF A SAVAGE I II III IV

A GANGSTA'S QUR'AN I II III IV

MURDA SEASON I II III

GANGLAND CARTEL I II III

CHI'RAQ GANGSTAS I II III IV

KILLERS ON ELM STREET I II III

JACK BOYZ N DA BRONX I II III

A DOPEBOY'S DREAM I II III

JACK BOYS VS DOPE BOYS I II III

COKE GIRLZ

COKE BOYS

By **Romell Tukes**

LOYALTY AIN'T PROMISED I II

By **Keith Williams**

QUIET MONEY I II III

THUG LIFE I II III

EXTENDED CLIP I II

A GANGSTA'S PARADISE

By **Trai'Quan**

THE STREETS MADE ME I II III

By **Larry D. Wright**

THE ULTIMATE SACRIFICE I, II, III, IV, V, VI

KHADIFI

IF YOU CROSS ME ONCE

ANGEL I II III IV

IN THE BLINK OF AN EYE

By **Anthony Fields**

THE LIFE OF A HOOD STAR

King Rio

By Ca$h & Rashia Wilson
THE STREETS WILL NEVER CLOSE I II III
By K'ajji
CREAM I II III
THE STREETS WILL TALK
By Yolanda Moore
NIGHTMARES OF A HUSTLA I II III
By King Dream
CONCRETE KILLA I II III
VICIOUS LOYALTY I II
By Kingpen
HARD AND RUTHLESS I II
MOB TOWN 251
THE BILLIONAIRE BENTLEYS I II III
By Von Diesel
GHOST MOB
Stilloan Robinson
MOB TIES I II III IV V VI
SOUL OF A HUSTLER, HEART OF A KILLER
GORILLAZ IN THE TRENCHES
By SayNoMore
BODYMORE MURDERLAND I II III
THE BIRTH OF A GANGSTER I II
By Delmont Player
FOR THE LOVE OF A BOSS
By C. D. Blue
MOBBED UP I II III IV
THE BRICK MAN I II III IV V
THE COCAINE PRINCESS I II III IV V
By King Rio

KILLA KOUNTY I II III IV

By Khufu

MONEY GAME I II

By Smoove Dolla

A GANGSTA'S KARMA I II III

By FLAME

KING OF THE TRENCHES I II III

by **GHOST & TRANAY ADAMS**

QUEEN OF THE ZOO I II

By **Black Migo**

GRIMEY WAYS I II

By Ray Vinci

XMAS WITH AN ATL SHOOTER

By Ca$h & Destiny Skai

KING KILLA

By Vincent "Vitto" Holloway

BETRAYAL OF A THUG I II

By Fre$h

THE MURDER QUEENS I II

By Michael Gallon

TREAL LOVE

By Le'Monica Jackson

FOR THE LOVE OF BLOOD I II

By Jamel Mitchell

HOOD CONSIGLIERE I II

By Keese

PROTÉGÉ OF A LEGEND

By Corey Robinson

BORN IN THE GRAVE I II

By Self Made Tay

King Rio

MOAN IN MY MOUTH
By XTASY
TORN BETWEEN A GANGSTER AND A GENTLEMAN
By J-BLUNT & Miss Kim
LOYALTY IS EVERYTHING
Molotti
HERE TODAY GONE TOMORROW
By Fly Rock

BOOKS BY LDP'S CEO, CA$H

TRUST IN NO MAN

TRUST IN NO MAN 2

TRUST IN NO MAN 3

BONDED BY BLOOD

SHORTY GOT A THUG

THUGS CRY

THUGS CRY 2

THUGS CRY 3

TRUST NO BITCH

TRUST NO BITCH 2

TRUST NO BITCH 3

TIL MY CASKET DROPS

RESTRAINING ORDER

RESTRAINING ORDER 2

IN LOVE WITH A CONVICT

LIFE OF A HOOD STAR

XMAS WITH AN ATL SHOOTER